Hi, My Name's Charlie

Joshua R. Burkheiser

Fulton Books, Inc.
Meadville, PA

Published by Fulton Books 2021

ISBN 978-1-63860-150-0 (paperback)
ISBN 978-1-63860-152-4 (hardcover)
ISBN 978-1-63860-151-7 (digital)

Printed in the United States of America

The world is a dangerous place to live; not because
of the people who are evil, but because of the
people who don't do anything about it.

—Albert Einstein,
as quoted in *The Harper Book of Quotations*
by Robert I. Fitzhenry, 1993

A psychopath is born; a sociopath is made.

Chapter 1

Your First (A Letter)

Hi, my name is Charlie.

Do you know that almost inescapable feeling you get when you're behind someone at the grocery store? The almost irrepressible urge to punch the person in front of you in the back of the head? There he is, talking to the cashier like he has known her all of his life. Counting out exact change or complaining about the raised price of milk. There you are, struggling to fight down the bubbling seething anger rising inside you. I think most people have felt this at some point. Now if you think about it from time to time, you can imagine that others have as well. That means while you're savoring the thought, the person behind you might also be imagining the same scenario. It's kind of terrifying when you think about it. Especially if the person behind you is someone like me…

I don't drink, gamble, or cuss. But I'm not without my vices; I do enjoy an occasional cigarette, but only after a big day. I'm friendly, courteous, honest to a point, and always smiling. It would seem like I was always a happy individual. But like beauty only being skin deep, that's where the act ends. To be honest, I'm miserable all day long, every day. I hate my job, my family, and my so-called friends. I spend hours staring at my computer screen at work trying to muster up the energy to complete the meaningless tasks that my boss keeps assigning me. I hate a lot of things, including myself, but above all else, I hate people. They are the single most disgusting and maddening creation that God unfortunately placed on this planet. We abuse each other, both sexually and emotionally. There is no other organism like us on the planet; we as a species stand here in ignorance, believing we are the most complex, intricate, and evolved structure, top of the food chain. We haven't even scratched the surface of how complex vegetation is in every form. Even moss is more evolved than we are. Everything people do drives me up a wall. If I could describe the sickening feeling I get when I walk through my city, I would, but I can't because it's so overwhelming.

Honestly, I wouldn't mind them too much if they just left me alone. Unfortunately, it's not part of the human condition to be unsocial. That feeling you get when you say hello to someone and they straight out ignore you is almost the same amount of anger I am surrounded with every day. But I understand people would think me odd if I stood in the shadows, wearing a black trench coat, shaking from rage for apparently no reason. So I paint a smile on my face and force small talk in an effort not to appear to be the next Unabomber.

I suppose that I should take this opportunity to describe myself, but I won't. I mean, I don't want you to have too clear of a picture of myself. That would be rather counterproductive, wouldn't it? I don't want to get caught anytime soon. I fit what so-called experts say the general attributes of a serial killer would be. I am a Caucasian, average height, and between the ages of nineteen and thirty-three. All in all, pretty unassuming. But that's where the similarities end. I am fairly social, enjoy normal meals; I even throw barbecues on occasion. I have no problem with any particular gender, race, or sexual orientation of other people. I even donate regularly to random charities. I vote…occasionally. I love animals and children and not in a creepy way.

Emotional abuse ran rampant in my family. All smiles on the outside but a bitter, sad existence for anyone on the inside. It was like a prison. I would avoid going home as much as possible, and when I did eventually make it home, I would hide in my room and submerge myself in the fantasy world of different authors. I dreaded my father coming home at night after work, his anger stemming from depression, all the while not realizing the emotional abuse my mother was torturing us with. Passive-aggressive complaints masked as some sort of weird statement about something worn or how we were performing. It builds upon a guy, though. It seems kind of tame, doesn't it? It wouldn't if you knew my parents.

My first signs of an anger issue probably stemmed from the age of eight or nine. I begged my dad for weeks to take me to the store to get a Rock 'Em Sock 'Em Robots game, that year's most popular toy for children. Every child had one; I had saved my allowance for months in an effort to get one, to be like the other kids in school. Counting the money every night over and over just to make sure that I had exactly enough change to bring that bad boy home. When we got to the store, I ran to the back of the Toys "R" Us and snatched the game off the shelf. Carrying it like a trophy up to register, I smiled, proud of myself, as the check-out girl ran it across the scanner. *Beep.* "$18.99 please," she asked, smiling. I handed her my entire jar of change. Now I know exactly how much was in there. I had made sure of it one last time before I left the house. "I'm sorry, you're ten cents short." Came back at me after she had counted the change. My face fell. She had made a mistake. I asked her to please count again, and she rolled her eyes, shaking her head as if I was the stupid one. She refused and set the game behind her register to put away later.

She pushed my change toward me, knocking almost half of it onto the floor, and then stood there sighing while, eyes full of tears, I struggled to pick up all of the change and put it back in the jar. The people behind me grumbled, pacing back and forth, angry that their busy lives had been waylaid by just a few minutes. I ran out to the car where my father waited and begged him for another dime. He angrily refused. Apparently, I had already wasted too much of his precious time. That began my lifelong hate of people. I know it seems like a small thing, but I almost didn't get to achieve a goal because this college dropout couldn't count? I have heard that life isn't fair, but why shouldn't it be? I spend my entire life trying to do the right thing, and I don't get to accomplish something because everyone else isn't even half-attempting. That's garbage and you know it. Don't sweat it; she's still living her poor excuse for a life somewhere. I mean I was a kid, and that wasn't that big of a deal. I don't kill just because I'm annoyed. I'm not a monster.

But I am going on a tangent, and I apologize. What I said in the beginning is not an exaggeration. There are other people out there like me who feel an uncontrollable pull in the pits of their souls to reach out and hurt someone. I think David Berkowitz (Son of Sam) said it best: "There are other 'sons' out there—God help the world." Now I'm telling you this, not to apologize for what I do but to warn you. I'm out there, I'm a killer, and I don't tolerate garbage.

My first kill was sloppy, I won't lie. I had just graduated high school, eighteen years old, and trying to make a go of it. Young at heart, innocent really. I angered easily, but I don't think I was any different from any other young man fighting to identify himself. I worked from sun up to sun down at a packaging factory, with dreams of eventually working up to management. It was hard work, and I barely scraped by financially. I never had extra money for myself. It all went to bills and food. On my days off, I usually lay around the house, exhausted from the week's workload.

This particular day was no exception. I woke up that morning without a care in the world. Hungry, I went to the refrigerator to fix up some eggs, only to find that I had run out sometime last week and had not bothered to replace them. Sighing, I grabbed the keys and headed for my car. That was probably my first mistake. Because had I just settled for a bowl of cereal, I probably wouldn't be writing to you right now. Kroger's was busy that day, too busy, but I managed to weave my way through the busy aisles full of annoyed mothers with their screaming children and snake the last carton of eggs. The lines to check out were exceedingly long, but I slowly moved through to the front of the line. After I paid, I counted the three dollars I had in bills. Depressing, really. I had to live off of three dollars till the next Tuesday. I walked through the automatic doors, and there he was. Do you know those homeless people who hang out in front of heavily populated locations and beg you for money? They sit there and milk you "to buy their next meal," all while holding an empty liquor bottle.

Now I'm not one to be swayed by vagrants, but once again, I was young and inexperienced. I knew that there were more unfortunate than I, and reluctantly I gave him the last change from the eggs in my pocket. The last of my money for that pay period. I watched him waddle away, the happiest man on earth. I walked back to my parking spot, feeling accomplished. Starting up my car, I realized that I was low on gas. I almost cussed. The factory wasn't within walking distance, and it's not like I could call off until after payday. My grandfather had given me a credit card for emergency purposes, but I didn't like owing him money because he had already done so much for me. But I didn't see how I had a choice. There was a gas station on the corner, so I swallowed my pride and headed in that direction. That was my second mistake; I could have made it home and enjoyed my eggs. I could have refueled anytime. But fate has an interesting way of taking your hand and molding your future.

Gas prices had risen that day. Ten cents! I remember choking back a swear word as I watched the price on the pump rise steadily higher. It's not like I made a ton of money just out of school. I angrily shook the last few drops out of the handle and headed inside to pay. The inside of the Shell station smelled faintly of refrigerant fluid. I find that most gas stations do. It's not really a bad smell, just an unfamiliar one. The line wasn't moving. I must have stood in that line for three minutes impatiently tapping my foot before I looked around the two people in front of me. And you know who was slowly counting out his ill-gotten pennies to buy a bottle of rum. I broke into a sweat watching him fumble through his pockets, slowly pulling out yet another of my coins. I couldn't believe it! I worked hard at a packaging plant to earn that joker's bottle of booze. Inside, I died a little bit. I could actually feel my stomach tied itself into knots, almost forcing me to cringe. Time slowed to an almost standstill, as he finally counted out the exact change and headed for the door. I numbly walked forward, with each step a labored breath. I couldn't believe the audacity! I was going to probably have to skip a few meals just so this guy could remain inebriated. "Sir? Sir?" the Middle Eastern man at the front counter asked, trying to get my attention.

"Yes?" I whispered, looking around. The people in front of me had cleared out after paying, leaving me standing alone at least two people's length from the counter. I walked forward and handed him my grandfather's card. I must have had a weird look when he handed me the receipt because he didn't bother saying the customary "Have a good day." I snatched the receipt from his hand and headed quickly to my car.

Lowering myself down in front of the wheel, I turned the keys with a sweaty palm. I should have just headed home, but I couldn't. I just couldn't. I needed to find him. I was like an addict; I couldn't stop myself. If I didn't do something, I would explode. I could feel it like air swelling up inside of me. I had to find a release. I followed him. He wasn't that far away. Just down the street, I found him tucking into a corridor behind a bowling alley. I parked the car in the parking lot, somewhat within the lines on the pavement, and followed him on foot. I know he didn't know I was there, but inside, I started imagining that he was running from me. It made me feel powerful, like some sort of wild animal stalking its unknowing prey. He continued down the alley until he got to the end and sat in the shade of a dumpster.

I swear I just wanted to confront him. I never intended anything else. He was so absorbed in getting off the wrapping around the cap that he didn't even notice when I approached him. I watched him for a few seconds, pondering what to do. He stood as I began screaming at him. We argued back and forth until he fell silent and shrugged his shoulders. My blood pressure raised to the boiling point, I turned to leave. That's when I felt the bottle hit the back of my head. Blood poured into my eyes as I fell to the ground. I curled into a ball and tried to fend off his kicking at my face. As I lay there trying to survive, blind rage and fear was replaced with a kind of resolution. This man had to die. He had to. I didn't have a choice. If I didn't, he would do it all over again. Besides, he was killing himself anyway. If anything, I would be doing him a favor. I was surprised at how easy it was working out in my head. The imagination is a powerful thing. I pictured myself overpowering him and doing whatever I wanted, molding the situation like Play Dough. I had almost completely run through the whole scenario before I realized that he was walking away assuming I had passed out. I slowly raised myself to my feet, wiped the blood and sweat from my eyes, and stumbled after him. I looked left and right until I found a piece of two-by-four that laid against the privacy fence. I gained speed as I jogged up behind him, raised the stud, and swung it with all of my might against the back of his head. His blood sprayed across my shirt, intermixing with whatever of mine that had dripped onto the front. He fell to his knees. I threw the two-by-four on the ground, walked around to face him, and bent to look him in the face. His breath reeked of decay and whiskey. I could feel bile rising up my throat. I choked it back down to avoid throwing up. And that was when it hit me. I knew exactly what I was going to do.

I reached down and grabbed him by the back of the head. Before he could react, my fingers curled around his disgusting greasy hair, yanking his head back to expose his yellow teeth. I searched for a weapon. He had dropped the open bottle beside his legs in an attempt to get a better grip on my arms. So, I reached down with my still free right arm and grabbed the bottle from the ground. If he wanted to drink, let him drink! I shoved glass neck of the bottle as far down his throat as I could, letting the brown liquid flow into his lying body. He started choking immediately, frantically struggling to find air. He stared up at me, clawing at my arms, drowning, the fear oozing from his pores. In one last attempt to find life-giving oxygen, he bit through the neck of the bottle, cutting his mouth to pieces. But it was too late for that. I let the last remaining few drops drip over the broken neck protruding from his open mouth and watched the last of his life leave his body. I could almost see his soul escaping his lifeless eyes. I held on to his hair for a little while longer, letting what I had done sink in.

Dropping him on the ground, I sat down letting the rush of adrenaline flow out of me. I felt so powerful, like God even. I had a choice to let a man live or die and had chosen correctly. Not many have ever known that feeling, and although the numbers will grow over the years to come, I relished the individuality of the moment. But I had to get my head on straight. There was much to do. That bottle had my fingerprints all over it. I jumped up from my sitting position and pried the neck of the bottle from his bloody mouth, cutting myself deeply on the jagged edge. This would later heal to leave scars on my palms. I wasn't sure if I had ever touched the neck, but I wasn't going to leave any evidence. I picked up the bottle from the ground and threw the neck into it. Then a thought occurred to me. I had given this man change; my prints would be all over the change in his pockets if he didn't spend it. I frantically searched his pockets for remaining change. Where was it? Surely, he had more change than he had spent on the bottle in the gas station. But finding none, I pulled his body from the ground and wrestled it over the edge of the dumpster beside him. Closing the lid, I headed back to the car with the broken bottle and two-by-four.

I started to drive back home when I was struck by yet another impulsion. A cigarette! I drove back to the gas station, removed my shirt, and wiped my face. Inside I smiled and asked the Indian guy for a pack of Golds. He nodded, saying nothing, but nervously grabbed a pack from above his register and rang me up. He must have noticed my hands were bleeding because he handed me a paper towel with my grandfather's credit card and watched as I carried my new addiction back to my car to drive away. Later, that was to be the first of many celebratory cigarettes. I let the smoke bend around my fingers as I smoked my death stick. Enjoying what was to be the first of many. A thought dawned on me that day. I had never been more content in my life, and I never wanted to forget it. That single thought began a unique collection for me. I pulled out my phone and took a picture of me smiling.

Now you have to understand I'm not a monster; I'm just tired of the garbage out there. There have been many since, but you always remember your first.

Sometimes I sadly think back on that day. I never did find out his name; I wish I had. The next morning's newspaper had only a paragraph, not even a valid attempt at covering his death, barely a shadow of what other murders in the city had. I like to think that everyone deserves a little more than that, even him. But society doesn't have a lot of feelings one way or the other. As long as it's not someone that they deal with on a regular basis. I got a little choked up that day; I'm a bit sentimental. Everyone should have a name. So I thought about it for a bit and decided on Charlie. It seemed to fit him, although I'm not sure why.

In case you're wondering, that's where I got the name at the beginning. Come on. You didn't think I was going to make it that easy to catch me, did you?

Enjoying our time together,
Charlie

Chapter 2

Father's Day

Hi, it's Charlie again.

I am so stoked today! Somebody is finally getting it! I was wondering how high the body count would have to grow before you all would start tying it all together. I mean seriously. Is there any other city in the world where they have over forty-nine murders per year? This morning's headlines had me on the edge of my seat. "Death with a vengeance?" Wow! You don't find writing like that anymore. I was so impressed I tipped the newspaper boy today! Of course, it's the holidays, so I imagine that most people did (in case you were thinking of asking the kids who had tipped them today).

In case you haven't caught that article today, it's about the drug dealer on the Upper East Side. I feel I should explain that one. It's not that I have a particular problem with drugs or the people that push them; it's the individual who you found and what he did.

I believe most people are good at heart, and so I try to look past the most inappropriate behavior, but some things can't be overlooked. Child abuse is one of them. There is nothing a toddler can do that should incite someone who is easily two hundred pounds his senior. I was abused as a child, and I did know a few children in my neighborhood that came to school with a couple of bruises here and there. I was always appalled that parents could do anything like that to their own flesh and blood. It was one thing to spank, but what possible reason would there be to close your fist and strike a child?

So when I was jogging through the park one morning last week, I was surprised to find a toddler sobbing on the side of the track. I slowed to look around for his parents. Not one adult was to be found in the area, so I approached him cautiously debating whether or not to call the police. "What's the matter, little guy?" I asked in a soothing voice. Raising his head, I could see the bruises that surrounded the left cheekbone. Only more sobbing. That's when I realized this child couldn't even form full sentences yet. He appeared to be no more than a year and a half old. I reached down and picked him up, trying to console his battered body. It took me probably three minutes before he calmed down enough to quit shivering. I set him down, stood back, and examined the child. Blond hair, tired eyes, and dirty clothing. I was reasonably sure his diaper had not been changed probably all night. Nobody should have to live like this.

I had started to dial 911 to report the little boy, when I noticed a man stomping toward us. This guy had to be 220, 230 easily. Dressed exactly how you would picture an inner-city thug would be. Ripped jeans pulled way down and sweat-stained wifebeater. The only thing that seemed out of place on him was his brand-new Jordan shoes. I find that to be an oddity. Why would you not purchase new jeans and wash your shirts before you purchased a brand-new pair of basketball shoes? But I digress. "Where the f——k have you been?!" the man screamed at the toddler, inciting yet another crying fit. I could feel the temperature rise on the back of my neck.

"Calm down, man," I said, keeping my voice even.

"Who the f——k are you?" he asked, turning his anger toward me.

"My name is Charlie," I told him and then tried to explain that I had run past to find the little boy crying, but he interrupted me before I could finish.

"I don't give crap. Mind your own f——ing business!" the man exclaimed, snatching the toddler by his arm and pulling him toward the street roughly. Rude… I almost ended my problem then and there, but that would have created a bit of emotional scarring for my new little friend.

I watched him walk off, shaking my head in disgust. I tried to follow his advice and mind my own business, but it was hard to shake off. His callous behavior toward his kid was making my pulse rise. I turned my back and started jogging back toward my car. I sat in my car trying to make sense of this world for quite a while. How could anyone do that to a child when there are people out there who would do anything to have one of their own? It's so unfair. My girlfriend and I have been trying to have one for over two years with no success. We have done everything we can, even considered in vitro, but the price was way too high. I may have risen up the chain at work over the years, but I still don't have $12,000 sitting around that we can spare. I would love to have children; I think I would be a great dad.

I woke up from my depression probably about twenty minutes later because my heart rate had calmed back down. The sweat on my shirt had dried. I shook my head and started the car. The roads back toward my house had gotten congested with traffic, so I decided to take a route through one of the neighborhoods that surrounded the park. Turning down Bostic Street, I began rolling up my windows. I'm not sure how other people feel when they drive through lower-income neighborhoods, but that is always my response. I think it might be partly a way of separating myself from putting up an albeit clear wall. I also believe that it is a way of blocking yourself off from feeling guilty. I shouldn't, but I do. I have worked hard to be where I am in life, and because of this, I live in a safer neighborhood. That thin glass pane between you and other people makes one feel like they are separate, even above feeling guilty.

I had just finished rolling up my window when I saw that same kid tied to a rope in the front yard of the house you found the body in. I slammed on the brakes, overwhelmed by a surge of emotions. That punk had tied his son to a fence post like a dog! I wouldn't, couldn't, just stand by and let this scumbag continue to walk this planet and defile this child's outlook on life. I'm not proud of this, but I couldn't leave this kid where he was. For the first time in my life, I became a temporary kidnapper. I jumped out of the car and untied the knots around his wrist. The knots were so tight they had started to raise welts around his wrists. A single tear ran down my cheek. How could he? I had never been that sad in my life. But I didn't have time for that then. I gently lifted the little boy into my arms and marched back to the car. I carefully strapped the seat belt around his waist in the back seat and started back down the road.

I drove around for an hour, trying to think of a safe place for him. It wasn't easy, you understand. I couldn't very well take him to the police station for obvious reasons, and it wasn't like I could take him anywhere that wouldn't cause people to ask questions. So I did the only thing I could do. I drove back to his house to put an end to you-know-who. On the way, I fell silent, trying to decide how to approach the situation. It had to be fairly quick; I had a toddler in the back seat. And I really felt like my kill had to fit the situation. What this man had done was unforgivable, sickening really.

I parked the car on a backstreet behind the man's house and handed the little boy my water bottle. Smiling, I patted his head and promised I would be back quickly. I don't think I will ever forget the look of appreciation that came over his face. This boy must have been starved for affection. I closed the door gently and turned sharply away. The fence in the backyard had become overgrown with vines, and it took a little bit to ensure I didn't place my hands in poison ivy. But I eventually found a clear space and lifted myself to the top. Dropping down, I found myself in waist-high grass. Was this guy serious? He couldn't find time in between beating his kid to mow his yard? I waded through the still-wet grass toward his back door, trying to decide exactly how I was going to handle my kill. I scanned the backyard to discover a baseball bat leaning against the shed in the corner. I changed my path and headed toward the rundown shed to grab the bat. My feet accidentally bumped the sidewall when I reached for the bat, causing the front door to swing open a little. And that's when I saw the purple light coming from inside. Curiosity got the better of me that day. And since you all would have searched the entire property by now, you know exactly what I found. Weed, growing all the way to the roof. The three bags in the corner were stuffed to the brim. I pushed aside one of the clumps of cannabis and let it fall back in place. I have never smoked marijuana, but I do know it's illegal and not in any way something you raise your kids around.

Disgusted, I turned to head back out of the shed when I noticed a single toy in the corner. A doll.

I don't know a ton about children, but I do know enough to understand boys don't often play with dolls if presented with other options. But I shrugged it off as poor parenting and headed back to the house. I pulled open the back-sliding door, careful not to make any noise. Stepping carefully through the kitchen, I almost vomited from the stench that rose from the dish-filled sink. There had to be at least three trash bags lining the farthest wall. As I turned the corner that led into the living room, I saw him staring at the television. In case you are wondering, no, he did not have a clue that his kid was gone. I know that on the surface, you probably don't agree with what I do, but deep down, I know that you appreciate me taking care of people like this. The bat fell with a satisfying thud across the back of his head.

He moaned and opened his eyes a few minutes later to find that his wrists were tied securely to the radiator in the living room by a piece of weed whacker cord I had found in the shed. I could see the fear rise as he struggled to scream for help over his mouth gag. I smiled knowingly. I understood what he was going through. The sudden realization that his life was about to end. A desperate muffled scream left his tape-covered lips. I have seen it at least a dozen times before then. I reached for the bat I had leaned against the wall and prepared to go to work. Just as I raised the bat above my head to a swinging position, I heard a soft groan coming from the back bedroom. I lowered the bat and crept down the hallway toward an open door. I carefully looked inside to find what I believe was a six-year-old girl tied to her bed with a blindfold on. This made the doll outside make more sense. I don't have to tell you the awful things that he did to her. I hung my head, overcome by an emotion I have never felt until that day settling over me. I covered her naked body. I wanted to set her free, but I didn't want her seeing my face or witnessing what was about to happen. I turned and slowly headed back to the living room blind with rage.

I know what you found in that back bedroom, and I will never get the picture out of my head. I still occasionally wake up crying at night. I want you to understand I had nothing to do with it. I hold the neighbors accountable for ignoring the screams that had to echo from that house. I also want you to know that the bloody shadow of a man you found felt every pain imaginable before he passed. He would never hurt someone like that ever again.

It took a full twelve minutes to ensure that he never saw the light of day. I started at his ankles, snapping each with every swing of the wooden bat. I then worked my way up. At each joint, I took careful aim, sometimes having to take several full swings. His collarbone was surprisingly hard to break. But with a little determination, I managed to break through. A dull popping sound came from his collar area. It was satisfying to know that above all the other bones, he would feel this one the most. Then thinking about the young girl in the backroom, I dragged my bat across his chest, down to his groin, and with every bit of strength I had, I let fly the bat. The inseam of his pants flooded red with blood. I sat back for a few moments to catch my breath, listening to his muffled sobbing. It's surprisingly tiring to do this line of work. I'll have to keep that in mind if I should ever do this again. I found myself wishing I had still had that water I gave the boy out in the car.

Smiling, I looked down at the battered body on the floor. The man had finally passed out, probably from the pain. I searched for something to wake him up but eventually just settled for slapping him back into consciousness. He groaned and rolled his tear-filled eyes back toward my face. I could tell it was starting to be too much for him. It was time to end this. I try to always observe the mercy rule when I can. I took the bat to his spleen just to make him feel it one last time and then, as you know, swung the bat down upon his head, severing the last thoughts of survival from his mind. I was surprised at the amount of blood that sprayed about the room. It went everywhere! The walls had little red dots all over. I watched amused as they turned from dots to lines running down to the floor. Artistic really. A sort of surreal beauty, deviant art if you will. I left him tied to the radiator and strolled to the kitchen to dial 911.

I waited until I heard an answer and let the receiver drop to the floor. I stopped just before the door and thought better of going back to the car with blood all over my clothes. I grabbed a set of clothes from the thug's dresser and went to the sink to wash up before leaving. I took careful notice to wash the bat clean. No point in freaking out the kid when I returned.

By now, Social Services had discovered who the boy's parents were and turned him over to the police. I called them and told them they could find him in the park and the girl in the backroom. *I kept an eye on him, from a distance, for you until they got there. You are welcome by the way. You won't find the murder weapon—it has been destroyed. And I wiped down all of the handles in the house, so unfortunately, there will be no fingerprints. Also, I laundered the clothing and hung it up in the park where you found the little boy. I'm not a thief.*

Please make sure that the children are taken care of. I have made an anonymous contribution to a charity that ensures that children of abusive parents are placed in loving families.

Tell him I'm sorry… Every boy should have a "good" dad.

Sadly, I can't end this letter on a happy note. That night, I couldn't even force a smile. I now have a picture of my face that reflects my dark mood, beside a lot of smiling ones.

Enjoying our time together,
Charlie

Chapter 3

Another Hunter

Hi, You-Know-Who again,

I noticed on the news the other day that you started looking into the killings. Good for you! I wish you the best of luck; I could use the exercise. I'm not going to lie; I'm starting to get a little excited. Today's article even quoted one of my letters to you. "I don't kill just because I'm annoyed." Even used my name. Wow! I can't believe you let that little gem out. Do you think that was smart? I mean, I imagine that people will read about the deaths and secretly support my decisions in their hearts. I don't care either way, but I didn't think you could release that kind of information to the public. I didn't mean for the general public to know about me. I was just letting you know a little about myself.

Also, I noticed that the newspaper stated that I had been responsible for the prostitute's death on Michigan Avenue last Friday. You should know I in no way did that. I wasn't even aware that it happened. I don't mind them misquoting me. But you should know you're looking for the wrong man. I wouldn't waste your resources following that lead thinking that it's me. I would never be caught with a prostitute. I am truly committed to my girlfriend. I would never cheat on her. Now I don't know if you have noticed this, but that isn't the only killing of prostitutes over the last three years. There have been several. When it first began, it happened like clockwork. Three murders every two weeks then nothing for twelve months. It's called a cooling-off period. And then another three over a two-week period. And then once again the same length of a cooling-off period. I would look into the National Guard or Reserve units here. They come down this way for training every year at about the same time. But most cooling-off periods are not that far apart. So this individual is probably killing in threes back in his own state as well. There, that should help.

Oh, and if you are going to quote me, let me see if I can give you something with a little bit more pizzazz! How about "Murder isn't an easy thing. It takes something (inside) that most people don't have. It's easy to imagine but harder accomplishing." How does that sound? I don't know; I'm not very good at this sort of thing. Manson was much better at this than I. But I do think it makes me sound a little hardcore. Feel free to make something up, something catchy.

I also noticed that the officer that was quoted called me a—and I quote—"sicko." I don't find that to be very professional. I hope to become a little more acquainted with him. Is there any way he could be placed in charge of the investigation? I feel like we would probably make a great team. Him chasing me, me eluding him. His name was Gershing. Thanks.

And in a sign of good faith, I would like to tell him a little more about myself. I was raised in a non-denominational church. I even attended church camp several times; those weeks were amazing. It really was good to get out in the summer air back in those days. I never will understand how kids can hang out inside their homes all day playing their game system. The other day, I went over to my neighbor's house to drop off their mail that had been accidentally placed in my mailbox. I rang and rang the doorbell until I eventually tired of waiting and looked through the glass on the front door. I could see their kid playing his Xbox, ignoring my presence on the front doorstep! Don't worry, he lives to play yet another day. But I did put their mail in their box. And yes, I did open their mailbox. I get it, federal offense. But I don't think that's the biggest of your issues right now. I just sighed and headed back inside to cook dinner.

My girlfriend couldn't join me that evening; she works late some nights. But nonetheless, I slaved over a hot stove in a futile attempt to bake a turkey. Have you ever tried to cook one of those? I swear I have no idea how mothers do that every year. It's harder than it looks. I tried to choke down the far-too-dry meat and gave up after the gravy did nothing to improve it. I ended up just making a sandwich and watching *Rizzoli and Isles*. By the way, not bad. I was impressed. When it first came out, it didn't sound that good. And every once in a while, they threw in an interesting plot twist.

Sorry, I trailed off again. Let's see... Work. Well, my job is a different story. It's long, boring, and it doesn't pay well. But the benefits are pretty decent. I get along with most of the people at work and honestly even find comfort in the stability of it. Although I still make sure to complain about it with my friends. I find that it helps fill in the gaps of conversation we sometimes find ourselves in. Plus complaining seems to be what draws people together in the workplace. It's not that I don't want to have deep conversations with them—I do. I just have a hard time relating to their generally pathetic topics of interest. It's always about what movies they have seen or who beat whom at whatever sport that is in season at the time. I hate sports. Don't you? It's so mundane. My dad would spend each Sunday engrossed in football. Mom would spend the whole day prior to getting together special dips and building intricately designed football-themed snacks. But instead of it being used as a family-building experience, the kids would be sent outside. Lord forbid that he actually spent some time explaining the game to us. Nowadays, it's gotten even worse; football games are shown on cable throughout the week.

Imagine my disgust when I found out my girlfriend was a college football fan. I make sure I am engaged in a chore during that time; it makes it easier than explaining that a man not only hates football but all sports in general. I honestly think that sometimes men and women just pretend to like sports to seem like everybody else. But I could be wrong.

Christmas is coming up! Got to love that. That is easily my favorite time of year, always has been. I can't believe how fast it snuck up this year. I have a lot of shopping to do! Thank God that Santa isn't real, right? I probably won't get many presents this year, am I right? I spend most of the year trying to hold back from singing

Christmas carols; my girlfriend hates it. But she does let me sing them as much as I want after Thanksgiving, so I have learned to tone it down until then. I haven't decided what to pick up for her yet. Maybe I'll swing by the ring shop.

We met the usual way. I had recently got out of a bad relationship and was looking for something new. My friend knew a girl who had the same thing going on and wanted to know if we want to get together. I was hesitant at first because friend-introduced relationships rarely panned out, but I was glad I gave it a chance when she stepped out of the car. It's actually a funny story. I had invited her out to the movies that night—you know, neutral ground and all that—and showed up a little early, dressed in khakis and a nice button-down shirt. I waited and waited, and just when I thought she had stood me up, I saw her cautiously approaching from the parking lot.

She had just gotten off work and hadn't had time to doll herself up any; as a matter of fact, she looked like she had driven there with the windows rolled down. But something about her drew me in. It was her eyes. The deepest sea of blue you have ever seen. When you stared into them, it felt like you were falling into a shadow. I was immediately and madly in love. I shook her hand and walked her into the lobby, making sure to hold the door for her. I paid for the next showing and took her hand as we walked to the concessions area.

I escorted her back to her car afterward, calculating the odds that she would let me kiss her. Not high, as it turned out. As she was searching for her keys to get in and drive away, I noticed a Taser in her purse! Smiling, I asked her why she had one of those. "Well, I don't know what kind of guy you are!" she replied, laughing. *You have no idea*, I thought to myself. But I chuckled under my breath and dug in my pocket for my knife. I pulled it out and extended it for her to see. "You take this. I would rather be stabbed to death than left on the ground convulsing," I said. I was being very serious, but she took it as a joke and placed it in her bag smiling. She still has that knife. And every time I see it, I think back to that first night and smile.

We have had many great moments like that since, and I truly hope many more will follow. She lights up life in a way that I cannot put into words properly. She is both my sun and my moon.

Charlie

Chapter 4

A Deadly Friendship

"You have got to be f——ing kidding me!" Officer Gershing exclaimed, angrily tossing the letter onto his desk. "This piece of garbage just doesn't get it! You can't just go around killing people because they are doing things that piss you off!" The other officers avoided his angry gaze. He was a bull in a china shop when he got in one of his moods, and few people had seen Gershing in this bad of a fit. He scanned the precinct for someone to vent too, but everyone had scattered in different directions, trying to look busy. Only one man had decided to stick around: Detective Chance Ronings. When Gershing finally locked eyes with Ronings, he was surprised to find them not falling away from his gaze. If anything, he looked amused, as if Gershing was some sort of child. Gershing stood up from his desk and stomped toward Ronings's office. It didn't take long for Gershing's large shadow to fill the office doorway. He stood there trying to look intimidating, but Chance was not easily cowered, especially by a pompous beat cop. Chance sat back and took Gershing in. At just over six feet, Gershing was no one to trifle with. Chicago born and bred, he had seen the rough side of life and had faced it with the same ferocity he was well known for. His face was scarred where an errant knife had cut him to the bone just above the left eye, or so the self-started story went... Chance chuckled a bit inside, thinking that he looked a little like Scar from Disney's *Lion King*.

Chance stood up slowly from behind his desk. "Is there something I can help you with, Gershing?" he asked in a slightly humored tone.

Gershing was taken aback. Most people visibly shrunk a bit when he was around, but Roning's voice wasn't even wavering. If anything, it seemed like he was taunting him. Gershing fumbled for something to say. "Uh…yeah. Why do you think that psychopath is targeting me?" he asked awkwardly.

"I haven't the foggiest," Chance said, shrugging his shoulders. But deep down, he had been asking himself the same question. He had tracked down killers for the past twelve years, and Charlie wasn't showing any of the same trademarks of a serial killer. It didn't make sense that he would single out a beat cop just for insulting him. Most serial murderers think they are above the rest of the world, somehow even Godlike at times. So it shouldn't have bothered Charlie that some pompous know-it-all beat cop trying to make a name for himself had called him a "sicko."

Gershing shoved his hands into his pockets and stormed back to his desk to sit down. While he was sitting there, a thought came to him. Why not try and catch this guy himself? It would make him famous—probably even get him into a detective position! The letter had mentioned him by name, almost calling him out. Gershing had never run from a fight, and this wasn't any different. If Charlie wanted a piece of him, then he was going to get it! Gershing pulled up Google and started researching the case, smiling.

Chance watched Gershing thoughtfully. He knew this much about younger officers: they were always trying to get ahead before their time. Maybe it was the stupidity of youth, or possibly life hadn't beat it out of them yet, but either way, this could pose a problem. The captain had already forbidden everyone there from investigating the Charlie case until the FBI from the Cincinnati office arrived. The FBI had taken all jurisdictions on serial killer cases back in the nineties, and they would be sore as hell if some beat cop had screwed up their evidence trail. He grimaced a little, remembering his last run-in with the FBI. Just four years before, Ronings had investigated a bank robbery just three blocks from the station. The three men had made off with over a quarter million dollars and twelve safety deposit boxes. Now it just so happened that one of the boxes belonged to the governor, who was quite fond of one of her necklaces that they had stolen. The investigation was going fine until her necklaces turned up in a local pawnshop. That's when the governor decided the investigation wasn't going fast enough. She called in the big boys to pick up where the police left off.

They came down like a tornado and wrecked the station with their equipment. And after three months of abusing the local police and looking down their noses at everyone, they got no further solving the crime and packed their bags to leave. They had even screwed up the Top Ten Wanted list paperwork, and the station had to correct that.

And it was all happening again. He had been told to pick up the agents who were to handle the case from the airport in the morning. He found it odd that they would fly in, considering that Cincinnati was literally less than an hour away. Chance rolled his eyes and chalked it up to the FBI's over-the-top showmanship at times.

His thoughts went back to Gershing. Charlie didn't seem like someone to screw with, and Gershing might be biting off more than he could chew. Chance wasn't sure what might come of the whole situation, but he was going to keep an eye on Gershing. The phone rang, and Ronings pulled himself out of his thoughts and answered it. "Detective Chance Ronings. How can I help you?" he asked.

"Chance? Chance Ronings?" a girl asked on the other end.

"Yeah. How can I help?" Ronings asked, a little confused as to how she would know his first name. It wasn't like it was listed on the phone extension.

"It's Aryn Bree-Wick! From high school!" the voice on the other end replied excitedly.

Chance frowned, trying to recall the name. It had been years since he had even let his mind even remotely fall back to his alma mater. "I'm sorry, I can't seem to place you," Chance answered bewildered.

"Oh, I'm sorry. It was Aryn Bree back then," Aryn corrected herself, trying to help out. But Chance didn't need any help. Now that was a horse of a different color. Aryn Bree wasn't easy to forget. Back in the day, she stood out like a sore thumb among all the rednecks that he had gone to school with. Long black hair had framed her ever jovial face. When she walked into a room, everyone's mood lifted. She was like a ray of sunshine. Every boy in that school wanted her, and every girl envied her. She had done everything from cheerleading to volleyball. She had even been a concert violinist if his memory served him.

"Oh yeah! Okay, now I place you. How have you been?" Chance asked.

"Well, actually pretty good lately. But this is kind of a surprise. I hadn't actually expected to talk to someone I knew!" Aryn told him. "I was actually calling in to see if I could get an interview with someone about the Charlie case. I work for the *Dayton Daily News* now."

Chance smirked a little. Newspapers and magazines had been calling all week to get an interview. It was actually getting a little annoying. Even if they had anything to tell them they wouldn't.

People don't realize it, but when information like that is leaked to the general public, it only hinders the investigation. "Well, I'm sorry to be the one who tells you this, but nobody here is allowed to talk about what we do know." Chance chose his words carefully. It wouldn't do to let everyone know that they honestly had nothing to go on.

"Oh... Well, that's okay. It was still cool to hear your voice again! We should catch up sometime! As a matter of fact, I'm free tonight. You should let me buy you dinner!" she asked, an obvious attempt to get an interview. Chance was still flattered, however, and he would like to eat something other than his own cooking for once.

"Sure. Sounds good, where should we meet?" Chance asked.

"I'll swing by your office when you finish your shift and pick you up! Oh, I guess I should ask, when do you get off?" Aryn asked.

Chance agreed and told her he finished his shift at eight, said goodbye, placed the phone back into its receiver. He leaned back in his chair and let his imagination take him. It had been a long time since he had been out to eat with a woman.

Eight o'clock was a long time coming. Chance spent the remaining three hours fielding domestic dispute phone calls and setting up interview times for different cases. It was tedious work, but in the end, it always left him feeling like he had done something good for the city. Not a lot of people can say that about their jobs. Finally, the shift was at an end. Standing up, he straightened his tie and threw back on his suit jacket. It felt odd to him; usually at the end of the shift, he was loosening everything and heading home to relax. Locking his door behind him, he took one last look around the office. Let his eyes trail over the other officers until they finally rested on Gershing. He was still there, hunkered over his computer screen. Chance's brow furrowed. Gershing's shift should have been over an hour ago. Shaking his head to clear it, he walked toward the front door. He could worry about Gershing tomorrow.

Aryn was right on time. She stood by the front desk, smiling and talking with the front desk officers. You could tell she was making their day. The men sat there all smiles; that was until Chance came around the front of the desk and she hugged him. Then they were nothing if not green with envy. And they had a right to be; the dress she was wearing was stunning. Long purple cloth hung in just the right places over her supple curves. Her exposed shoulders were smooth and tan, and draped around her neck was a matching colored piece of glass hanging from a simply braided cord. She was unbelievable. She had matured into a beautiful woman. It made him wish he had built up enough courage when he was younger to ask her out. She smiled sweetly and asked him if he was ready to go. Assuring her that he was done for the evening, she wrapped her arm around his and guided him out into the night, leaving the front desk cops staring in disbelief.

Once they had gotten to her car and she started up the engine, Chance complimented her dress and asked her where they were going. "It's a surprise!" she told him, smiling. After a little prodding, he managed to get out of her that it was about ten minutes away. He settled into the seat and relaxed. His stomach was growling. He only lived about a block from the station, so it didn't take him long to walk home, and his stomach knew it was time for his usual hot pocket and glass of milk. He watched the people mill about the busy street as they passed, but try as he might, he couldn't get out of cop mode. It had made him suspicious of everyone. Each person he passed, he was steadily trying to decide what they were up to. He shook his head and looked at the clock. Twenty minutes had gone by! Aryn apparently had no sense of distance! He smiled but, wisely, said nothing. Finally, she pulled in front of Les Frères Heureux (The Happy Brothers). He had heard a lot about the French restaurant but didn't have the cash flow to ever actually dine there. He suddenly felt underdressed even in his suit. The valet opened Aryn's door and helped her step out. Her lithely form framed in the doorway made his heart skip. She was truly a beauty like no other. She traded the attendant a numbered tag in exchange for her keys, and they walked inside.

"Bonjour, madame. Do you have a reservation?" the maître d' asked.

"Yes, it's under Bree," she told him, smiling. It might have been his overactive imagination, but it appeared like she was stressing that she wanted Chance to think of her as the girl he used to know. But he let it pass as they were escorted to their table by the window overlooking the city. She had pulled out all of the stops for the night, that was for certain. She probably had a newspaper credit card tonight, he thought dryly.

She began looking over the menu, and Chance took this time to start a relaxed conversation. Everything he had rehearsed in his head earlier that day had been forgotten. "Um…so what have you been up to since high school?" Chance asked, at a loss for anything else. She looked up and smiled warmly.

"Well, it's really not that much to tell. I went to college in Seattle and then bounced around from magazine to magazine until I finally got a job offer out here working for the newspaper," she told him, shrugging her shoulders.

Chance could tell she was leaving a big part of her story out and his interrogation skills jumped in naturally. "I noticed you have a new last name," he said almost nonchalantly.

Her face grew red, but she quickly recovered and smiled. "Now, Detective Ronings, I believe you're off work right now."

Chance acknowledged her reluctance with a smile but did tell her that he was sorry and that it wasn't something you could just drop.

"Really? Do you mean to tell me that I'll be dining with a cop tonight and not an old friend?" she asked, kidding him softly, almost purring. The waiter came by just in the nick of time. Chance let her order first and just asked for the same thing. He didn't really understand any of the menu and was really more of a cheeseburger-and-fries kind of guy. So instead of embarrassing himself further, he just hoped she didn't order snails.

Aryn sipped her glass of water and looked Chance over. It had been years since she had seen him last. The years had been kind. Years of exercise and tracking down criminals had shaped him into a muscular, hard-looking man. A far cry from the scrawny boy he used to be. His blondish red hair fell carelessly across his forehead, framing his deep grayish-blue eyes, making them appear even darker. Though he had some light scars on his chin, they seemed to tell a sort of story. A story that she wanted to know. "So you're a detective now. How did you end up this far away from home?" she asked.

"Well, it's a long story, but the short version is, I met a girl, traveled with her, it didn't work out. But fortunately, the police force out here adopted me," Chance told her dryly. It wasn't the whole story, but it was the highlights. Some scars are not visible; some are on the heart. She related to the story much more than she would like to admit. She, too, had followed somebody out here and had her heart wrenched out of her. He didn't need to say it; she could read it in his soul. The way only one who had had the same thing happen to them could see it. Her eyes welled up with tears a little, and she leaned across the table and rested her hand on his. Their eyes met, and for a second, no words needed be spoken. They both could feel the pain shared. Chance was the first to recover, drawing his eyes away, and scanned the room for his rescuer, the waiter. Unfortunately, he was nowhere to be seen. Looking back at Aryn, she, too, had composed herself and seemed to be searching for something to say.

"You were saying that you had a hard time turning off the police mode? In what way?" she asked.

Chance, relieved to have a new topic, happily tried to explain. "Well, I'll give you an example. Do you remember the valet? He was scanning your car for loose items that he could steal while you were inside. Loose change, possibly earrings. Whatever he could lay his hands on. And the guy taking our reservations? He isn't French at all. You can tell because his accent is too thick. He is overcompensating. A foreigner would have less of an accent because he would be trying to fit in. It's the same as when you meet somebody from the south and after a little while, you catch yourself developing a twang."

She seemed doubtful, so Chance explained further.

"Also, when you called today, you knew I would be there. I know that because if you had called the front desk and just asked to talk to someone about the Charlie case, they would have transferred you to the captain. So that means you would have had to have asked for me by name." He looked at Aryn for a sign he had insulted her, but she seemed even more intrigued.

"Wow! That's amazing! You are one hundred percent right! I did know you were there. I shouldn't have lied to you, I'm sorry. It's just my job. I am still trying to get that story." She looked chastened after admitting it, however.

Chance suddenly felt awful about calling her out on the deception. "Hey, it's no big deal. Let's just enjoy the night. If you want, we can talk about the recent murders. I doubt it will help, but I will tell you what I can. But my name stays out of it."

Aryn seemed elated by this and got out a pad of paper and a pen. "Oh, thank you! This means a lot. Um, I'm not even sure where to start. Does Charlie really kill people that annoy him, or is it just bad people?" she asked, the eagerness making her voice tremble.

He told her what he could about the killings, even the letters, minus anything that wasn't already known by the general public. But then he tried to explain that Charlie wasn't someone to be admired or looked up to. He was still breaking the law. After giving her the information that he could over dinner he asked her to not write Charlie into a hero role. "Charlie is not a superhero. He isn't Batman. He is just a killer."

When dinner was complete and the valet had brought around the car, minus some loose change, Chance pulled him aside and offered him twenty bucks to answer a simple question. "Hey, man, settle a bet for us. I think the maître d' is actually from France, but the lady thinks that he is from New York. Who is right?"

The waiter grinned and admitted he was not from France. "No way, man. France? That hombre is from Alabama!" The valet walked away laughing and shoved the twenty into his vest pocket. Chance smiled and winked at Aryn and got into the passenger side. Aryn shook her head in amazement and followed suit. They laughed all the way back to Chance's street.

As she pulled up in front of his apartment, she began to look worried. "You live here?" she asked.

Laughing, Chance assured her it was a lot nicer inside. "If you have time, I'll show you around." She shyly laughed and agreed. He stepped out, walked around to the other side of the car, and opened the car door for her. She looked up and smiled, recognizing manners when she saw them. She followed him up the stairs to his apartment, being careful not to trip in her high heels. When he finally opened the door, she was amazed to find that he was not exaggerating. It looked like a penthouse suite. Lush gray carpeting covered the floor, leading up to a panoramic view of the city lights. It was intoxicating. He stood back and watched as she soaked in the view.

"You still have it," he told her.

"What?" she asked breathlessly.

"You can still light up a room," he said, winking. Walking off toward the kitchen, he raised his voice. "Would you like something to drink?"

"Um, wine would be great!" she called back.

He chuckled and leaned against the kitchen entranceway. "Will a beer be okay?" he asked.

She smiled and nodded. As he went back in to get the beer, she pressed her palm against her head. Why would she assume that he had wine? He's a bachelor. "I hope I didn't offend you. I don't know why I thought you would have wine," she told him when he had handed her a beer.

He shrugged and sat down. "No big deal. I'm just sorry I'm not better prepared for the company." She laughed and sat down beside him. For a while, they just sat there and talked about old times, staring off into the night. Before she realized it, she found herself leaning against him. There was something comforting and familiar about him. His aftershave still faintly clung to his neck from the morning shave. Feeling his muscle beneath his shirt both aroused her and brought her back to reality. She straightened up and smoothed her dress.

"So we should do this again sometime!" she told him. "I had a great time tonight!" She started to stand when he pulled her gently back down.

"How about tomorrow night?" he asked, surprised by his own forwardness. The only thing he knew was that he didn't want this night to end. She looked into his eyes and was drawn in by their intensity.

"Okay" was all she could muster. She drew closer to him and brushed his lips with hers. Both of their hearts beat faster until finally, Chance could stand it no longer and kissed her hard on the lips. She was lost in the heat of the moment and only stopped to catch her breath. Trying to regain her composure, she lightly pushed away.

"I really should be going," she almost whispered.

"Well, you have been drinking," Chance said, still under her spell.

"Yes?" she asked, quivering.

Chance drew her close and said in a low voice, "What kind of cop would I be if I let you drive home tonight?"

Chapter 5

The Game Begins

Chance's eyes fluttered open. His mind still numb, he rolled over and stretched his stiff body across the sheets. It took him several seconds to realize that Aryn was no longer beside him. He sat up slowly and tried to focus his eyes to look for some sign of the brown-eyed beauty. Finding no one, he stepped out of the bed, grabbed his pants off the dresser, and headed to the living room. It had been a long time since he had entertained at his apartment, but he was pretty sure that after spending the night with someone they were supposed to say good morning to you or, at the very least, goodbye. Not finding her in the living room, Chance rolled his eyes and sat down heavily on the couch. He hated starting off his day in a bad mood. The sun was rising over the city's skyline and flooded the apartment in a warm white glow. He sat back and reflected on last night.

Waking up to an empty house, the events that had transpired throughout the previous night seemed to be more like a dream. He hadn't spent the evening with a woman for a very long time, and it bothered him that she hadn't stuck around long enough to say goodbye. It made him feel cheap. It was partly his fault that it bothered him so much, however. Every time he made love to someone, he gave a part of himself to them. Even though they had spent only a few hours last night on their date, he had become emotionally tied to her. In the bedroom, his clock alarm went off. The incessant buzzing dragging him out of his solemn meditation. Chance sighed and walked sluggishly to the bathroom to get ready for his day.

Letting the warm water run down his back, he tried to clear his head, but it was impossible. It didn't seem fair she could be that callous, but after all, what did she owe him? It's not like they had made plans for the next day or even discussed seeing each other again. One passionate night shouldn't lock someone into anything they don't want to be in, he supposed. It wasn't like it was the 1920s or anything. Gone are the days of courtship. Long hours of just sitting on the porch, getting to know someone simply because you were told that was the proper way to do things by your society or your parents.

Deep down, he knew was just trying to make himself feel better. Grumpily, he scrubbed and rinsed himself off. Stepping out, he was just in time to hear the phone ringing in the living room. Throwing a towel around his waist, he ran to answer it. "Hey, Ronings! Heard you went on a date last night!" The voice on the other end was Captain Rashan Murphy, Ronings's boss and longtime friend.

Chance laughed. "Is there anything you don't know, Rashan?" Rashan's last name was Irish, and it always confused people when a six-foot-two aging black man reached out to shake their hands. Chance smiled good-naturedly and waited to find out why he was calling.

"Hey, I sent Officer Gershing to pick the feds up from the airport. I need you back here ASAP! We got another letter. Charlie isn't playing games this time. He isn't happy about this morning's paper," Rashan said, getting serious.

"What paper?" Chance asked the captain. But he already knew. Aryn hadn't left for no reason. She had a deadline to meet. And that deadline was today! After the captain and he had said their goodbyes, he threw on his clothes in a hurry and ran out the door, steaming that he had been played so skillfully.

The walk was a short one, and he was in a hurry to get to the precinct. It only took him ten minutes to get from his apartment to breeze past the front desk. The entire office was in an uproar. People were flying all around, and several of his fellow detectives were crowded into the captain's office.

"How did this even happen!" Rashan roared. "Who was it? It had to be somebody here!" Apparently, he was in captain mode, Chance mused. The whole office fell silent. You could have heard a pin drop.

"It was me," Chance spoke up.

The captain's eyes widened and his nostrils flared. "Get out! Get the f—— out! Everybody except Ronings!" Rashan yelled, pointing at Chance. The detectives pushed past him in a hurry to be out of the firing line. Chance closed the door as the last one filed out.

"What the hell happened, man?" Rashan asked excitedly.

"Well, I went on the date last night, and it turned out that she was a reporter," Chance confessed gloomily. Rashan leaned back in his chair and rubbed his eyes. He had seen a lot of stupid people in his days on the force but he found it hard to believe that Chance was one of those people.

The captain snatched the paper off his desk and asked. "Do you mean to tell me that you told her that, and I quote, 'I'm going to catch this SOB if it's the last thing I do'?" Throwing the paperback in a heap on his desk, he stared incredulously at Chance, waiting for an excuse.

Chance, confused, reached over and grabbed the paper off Rashan's desk. Scanning the paper, he was surprised to see the article read more like a piece of fiction than actual news. His eyes fell on the author's name. Sandra Lemont. Chance looked up, grinning slightly. It wasn't her! She hadn't written the article! Rashan's face was turning red, too shocked to find words. Chance had just admitted telling this woman he was going to personally hand Charlie his ass. And he was smiling? Chance, noticing Rashan appeared about to lose his mind, decided it was time to clue the captain in. "Boss, I didn't tell this woman anything. I went out with a girl named Aryn last night, and I didn't tell her anything that you hadn't approved everyone here to say."

Captain Murphy's face started to turn from a deep fiery red back to a normal skin tone and then slowly back to red again. If Chance hadn't said anything to this reporter, then who did? Rashan leaned back in his chair and composed himself. Chance pulled a chair up in front of his old friend's desk. "I don't know who did talk to this chick, but it wasn't me," Chance told him, waiting for a response. Getting none, he continued, "You said Charlie wrote again?"

Rashan pulled an evidence bag from under the newspaper and threw it in front of Chance. "It's right there. The devil of it is, this guy has managed to drop this thing off on three different officers' doorsteps, and no one's seen him do it! It's like he knows where we all live!" Rashan said, exasperated.

Chance held the letter thoughtfully. It was true that Charlie seemed to know a lot about the inner workings of this office. It could mean that someone here was unintentionally letting information out, perhaps to a friend or family member, or even that someone was helping him from the inside. Unfortunately, because of the internet, anyone with a computer and some initiative could find at least some of that information. Chance read each word carefully. His forehead furrowed with concern. The message was short and very clear!

FIND THIS COP BEFORE I DO!
—CHARLIE

He couldn't put his finger on just what it was, but something about it looked off to Chance. He looked at Rashan. The old captain's face read like an open book. His old friend cared for each of his officers like they were his own children. And a threat against his precinct was a threat against his family. "Who found this?" Chance asked, trying to draw Rashan back into the game.

Rashan shook his head to clear it and said, "Umm, Gershing did actually. That's why I sent him to pick up the feds. I'm putting him on their team during the investigation."

Chance sat back abruptly and took that in. Was it possible that Gershing had composed this whole thing just to be a part of this investigation? He had spent all day on his computer instead of being on the streets like he was supposed to be. Was he even that smart? Chance didn't know what to think about the news, but he knew he didn't like it. "I'm assigning you to lead the investigation from our side and assist wherever they need you. Pick your team and get back to me." Rashan's voice cut through Chance's thoughts. Chance pondered on what his boss told him; he hadn't even contemplated being a part of this whole thing. Chance usually worked alone and didn't relish the idea that he would have to work in a group.

"I'll take Pullman, Merrings, and Truman," Chance told Rashan after a few moments.

"All right, well, get out there and let them know. The feds will be here pretty soon," Rashan said dismissively.

Chance had just got up and turned the knob to walk out of the office when Rashan said, "Oh, and Chance. Bring this guy down before he gets anyone else!" Chance nodded solemnly and closed the door behind him.

Wasting no time, Chance called the three detectives he had chosen into the office and closed the door. All three of them stood there with sheepish grins, obviously still under the impression that Chance was the one who had given the reporter the story. Chance explained what had transpired in the captain's office and sat back to let them absorb the whole situation. He made it a point to keep his suspicion of Gershing out of it, however, and sat back to answer any questions.

"How much do we know about Charlie?" Merrings asked. Merrings had been working with the Dayton police for a little over three months; before that, he had worked with the Chicago PD and had already made a lasting impression on everybody he had met. A short but athletic young man, his attitude made up for his stature. As a matter of fact, if someone was asked as to how tall he was, without him being around, they would swear that he was at least three inches taller than he was. Always pleasant and quick with a compliment, he was an all-around nice guy. A stark contrast to his two companions. Pullman was tall and rotund, a stereotype detective if there ever was one. He looked a little like William Conrad (Jake and the Fatman). Years of stakeouts and fast food had shaped him into a very fat and moody individual. But what he lacked in physical prowess he made up for in intelligence and street smarts. Chance respected him very much. And lastly came Truman. Daniel Truman was the last of a dying breed. A true man in every sense of the word. He took crap from no man and didn't give any unless goaded into it. When Chance had shown up at the precinct a rookie, Truman had put him under his wing. It took several years, but Truman had molded Chance into the detective he was today. Above all the others, Chance valued his expertise and advice.

"Well, according to his letters, we know that he is between 5'8" and 5'11", Caucasian, and between the ages of nineteen and thirty-three. Other than that, Charlie appears to have above-average intelligence. Oh, and he probably works at an office job associated with some sort of factory." Chance read off the bio to the detectives.

Merrings nodded and jotted down notes.

"I need you guys to go over the letters and the cases that we know he was responsible for. Also, get with the guys from records to try and weed out any others he might be a suspect for. I'll get back to you again after I talk to the guys from DC."

Pullman nodded and grabbed Merrings by the arm to get him headed to the door. Before Truman had the opportunity to follow suit, Chance asked him to hang back. "I would like to run something past you."

Chance stood up, walked to the other side of his desk, and leaned on it. "I think we might have a problem with the other officer on this case," Chance said flatly.

Truman shrugged his shoulders but said nothing.

"It's Gershing. The captain assigned him to the case, mainly because of his involvement in the last case and now because of him receiving this letter. I'm just afraid he might have leaked the story to the press," Chance told Truman. He went on to explain his suspicion that the letter may not even be from Charlie but might be written by Gershing himself.

Truman listened, mulling over Chance's suspicion carefully. Several minutes passed before he put his thoughts into words. "Well, you might be right. I wouldn't put it past him. But you should probably keep him around. He might come in useful later. But I'll keep an eye on him just the same." Truman said in his deep, gravelly voice. Chance thanked him, knowing what that meant. When Truman said "keep an eye on him," he meant that he wouldn't let Gershing out of his sight. Gershing probably wouldn't like it, but he might have dug himself into a grave that only Truman could pull him out of.

Just as Truman had said his goodbyes and headed toward the file room, Gershing appeared with the agents from the FBI. Both agents were dressed basically the same and had identical Bluetooths attached to their ears, but that was where their similarities ended. The first agent was probably in his fifties and stood tall with silver hair. Wrinkles showing his obvious experience with the department. His entire demeanor demanded respect. Following him was one of the youngest agents Chance had ever seen. It looked like they had recruited the guy straight out of high school. Acne still clouded his youthful face, and eagerness shined in his eyes. He carried simply a computer case and an overnight bag with the airline tag still attached to the handle. Gershing marched up to the captain's office with a smile on his face.

Chance rolled his eyes, sighed, and walked back to his office. Chance closed the door behind him and looked around the room. Photos and citations adorned the four walls. Different people and memories from Chance's past life. There were many awards, but the largest frame held the Medal of Valor, the highest award that an officer of the law can earn. As Chance's eyes fell over it, his shoulder started to ache. It had been years since that day, but he remembered like it was yesterday. It was his rookie year on the force, and Chance had been on foot patrol for just over seven months. Chance was directing traffic in the center of downtown when a shot rang out across the city square. The echo was so bad it was hard to tell in which direction it came from. Chance scanned the storefronts hoping to find something out of place to no avail. Grabbing his radio transmitter, on his left shoulder, he called in the gunshot to dispatch. The reply was immediate. A few minutes before the gunshot, a 911 call was placed by a woman. She described what looked like an altercation behind a drug store on Second Street, just one street behind Chance's location.

"I'm on it. Send back up to that location, officer going in on foot," Chance told dispatch, as he started running toward Second. Few officers were assigned downtown in the city's bustling center; most were sent out to patrol the surrounding suburbs. He knew that backup was probably several minutes behind him. As he approached the drug store that the 911 caller had described, he noticed something odd about the cars parked in front. Two of the cars were parked southbound on a one-way street running the opposite direction. Chance stopped outside of the door, just long enough to catch his breath, and pushed open the door, weapon drawn. He could feel his body kicking into overdrive. Something happens to your body when you face a life-and-death situation. High-level sympathetic nerve stimulation during a fight-or-flight reaction causes the adrenal medulla to release a large bolus of adrenaline and norepinephrine into the bloodstream. Your blood carries the hormones to your body organs and tissues, where they attach themselves to receptors and achieve the fight-or-flight response. He had a decision to make, but in many ways, he had already made it.

This was the first time that Chance had actually removed his pistol from its holster since he had joined the force and was a little hesitant in its use. He would learn to regret this. As Chance stepped through the doorway, a little bell attached to its frame rang. As his training dictated, he lowered his height, ensuring a smaller target. Creeping forward, he cautiously scanned the isles. Chance could feel beads of nervous sweat drop down the small of his back under his body armor. His heart raced violently in his chest, and his breathing quickened. Never before had he been faced with the possibility of death, and he didn't like it. As Chance neared the front register, he stopped for a moment to compose himself and looked over the top of the counter. Chance swallowed hard, trying to keep his stomach from emptying. Two young girls were lying in large pools of blood. Chance flipped the safety on his weapon and turned sharply away. He didn't know why, but he was mad! Two young girls gunned down before they even reached their prime! And probably over a few bucks that was kept in the register! Chance shook his head and headed for the front door to call it in. But a muffled sound in the back room made him stop abruptly. He cursed silently, angry with himself that it hadn't even occurred to him to clear the rest of the building. Chance spun on his heels and walked to the back door. As silently as he could, he pushed the heavy door open just enough to look inside. Two men were hunched over what appeared to be a safe. Chance should have walked back outside that day and called it in. That would have given his backup enough time to arrive, and the two men might have been brought in safely. All of his training had taught him to do this, but Chance had forgotten all of it. Blinded by the rage of finding those two girls, he threw open the door and yelled, "Police, freeze!" Both men were taken by surprise but were quick to react. As the men drew their weapons, Chance squeezed the trigger. *Click, click...*

Chance had forgotten to take the safety off of his pistol! The room thundered with gunshots. Chance was pounded to the floor as the rounds sunk into his armor. The men jumped over him and ran toward the front of the store. By pure adrenaline, Chance pulled his body off the ground and ran after them, gasping for air. The men had made it to the street as Chance billowed through the front door. The taller of the two men spun around to confront him. The man smiled as he looked down the sights at Chance. Time froze for Chance in that split second, and he raised his gun. Like a legendary gunfight in the old west, he quickly fired from his waist and fell to his knees. Chance's first bullet caught the man in his neck and his second on the man's right hip, throwing off the man's aim. As he fell to the ground, his finger pulled the trigger. A split second before Chance heard the round fire out of its chamber, his right shoulder exploded in a spray of blood, throwing him against the wall. The second man's eyes grew wide, and he jumped into the driver's side of his car. Throwing himself in reverse, he slammed on the gas to get away. An approaching truck slammed into the front of the car, sending the driver careening forward. Sirens screamed down the street surrounding the getaway car. Pulling himself back on to his feet, Chance staggered toward the jumbled mess of police cruisers. Rashan was there, screaming something at him, but Chance couldn't hear him. The adrenaline had taken over his body, deafening him to the surrounding world. Chance's pistol sights drew level on the approaching car. One thought, and one thought only, thundered through his mind: End it. Few men have been faced with the choice of killing, but all men have the ability. And Chance had made his decision. Just as Chance's finger squeezed the trigger, he was bodily thrown to the ground. He hit the street, heavily slamming his head against the pavement. The world around him darkened as his eyes closed, fading out the light of day.

Chance spent the next three days in the hospital with fluids and blood being piped into him. It wasn't until after those three long days that he discovered what had happened. Rashan had grabbed him just before the car would have struck him. He owed the old captain a life debt. After two months of medical leave, he found himself standing in front of the mayor receiving the Medal of Valor. Rashan had left out the part where Chance had attempted to end the life of the second robber.

Loud knocking on his door snapped him back to the present day. As the door opened, Chance turned to face Gershing. "Hey, boss, the captain filled me in. I guess I'm working for your team on this case." Chance grimaced but nodded in acknowledgment. "Okay, so cool, where do you want me?" Gershing asked impatiently to start.

"The other guys are down in the record room. Go ahead and meet up with them. They will explain what's going on," Chance ordered. Gershing shook his head enthusiastically and walked briskly toward the elevator.

With a sense of dread, Chance watched him walk away. He did not want Gershing involved with this case whatsoever, but it was too late to stop him. He leaned against the frame of the door, pondering what he should do about Gershing, that was until he noticed Rashan making a beeline toward him with the two feds in tow. "Detective Ronings! These are the gentlemen that DC sent over to head the Charlie case," Rashan said smiling. Rashan made the introductions and then excused himself, ensuring that he was leaving them in good hands. The older of the two was named Tom Black and was the lead investigator. His young compatriot was named Dr. William Tuttle, but Tom affectionately called him Turtle. Chance wasn't sure why but declined to ask. Turtle was the psychologist for the Cincinnati office and was assigned to the case based on previous successes in using psychologists in serial killer cases. After sitting the two agents down on the couch facing his desk and getting them both some coffee, Chance returned to the cheap leather seat behind his desk. Tom took a sip of the hot black concoction and grimaced. "Wow! This has a kick!" He smiled politely and set down the coffee on the end table beside him.

Chance chuckled. "Yeah, the guys here work pretty late shifts and tend to make it a little stronger then Maxwell house intended." Turtle smirked and took a big gulp but kept silent. Chance waited for one of them to start talking, but they seemed to be content letting him guide the conversation. So Chance began. "Well, I'm not sure how much you know about this case, but I would be happy to fill you in with what we know up to this point." Tom nodded and got out a digital recorder. Pressing a few of the buttons, he set it down and pointed in Chance's direction, indicating that he could start anytime. Chance began from the first letter, making sure not to leave out anything. Handing over the letters as he went along, the agents took them and scanned over them. Turtle pulled out a small wand-like scanner and ran it over each page.

When Chance had finished, Tom leaned over and shut off the recorder. "I think that you might be holding something out on us, Detective Ronings," Tom said blandly after a few moments. Leaning back in his chair, Chance took a few seconds before answering. "There is a possibility that the last letter is a fake. The officer that brought you in today has been on my radar for a little while. I believe that he may have written it himself after singing to a local paper today about Charlie. I don't know why he would, but I honestly suspect that he just wanted to be a part of this investigation. Maybe for notoriety, maybe for a promotion, but whatever the reason, Gershing is more of a liability than an asset." Tom crossed his legs, and a thoughtful look clouded his face. Other than the loud slurps that came from Turtle drinking his coffee, the room had fallen silent.

A few minutes passed before anyone spoke. Tom was the first to break the silence. "Well, I appreciate the briefing, but I think we both could use a little sleep. We flew in from another assignment and haven't caught our second wind yet. The captain told us that your guys were in the records room dragging old cases together, so I guess we should probably go check into our hotel."

Chance nodded and stood to shake their hands. "I'll send a patrol car around to drive you. Do you want to pick this up in the morning? Say seven?" Chance asked. They readily agreed and headed toward the front of the precinct. He watched them go, wondering just how this whole thing was going to shape up.

Chance joined the rest of the team down in the records room and started sorting through unsolved cases. The stack had already grown to a fairly large mountain, and Gershing was separating them by dates. The men had tried to limit them down to the last twenty years and only in the local area. Based on Charlie's letters, he indicated that the murders were very brutal, so they also tried to separate the milder cases from the most violent. This went on for hours with the pile growing, and the team was growing restless. After finally narrowing down the records to just a few potential murders, Chance stood to his feet and stretched. "All right, guys, go home and get some rest, tomorrow we are kicking off this show at seven." Chance told them. The guys nodded and left, thankful to be done with the musty, dark records room. Locking the door behind him, Chance headed toward the front door to head home.

The walk home was dark and cold. Fall had set in, and the winds were not being kind. It tore through Chance's jacket and made him shudder. Pulling the collar of his jacket up to block the wind from the back of his neck, Chance leaned into the wind and sauntered on. The street lights overhead flooded the pavement in a warm orange glow. As people passed by, they would give a courteous nod and continue on their way. Oblivious to the fact that Chance was one of seven men who were tracking down a killer that preyed on these very streets. Climbing the steps up to his apartment building, he paused shortly to grab his mail before heading in. Chance thumbed through the bills as he walked up the carpeted steps inside. Chance reached for the doorknob without looking and grasped at empty air. Chance looked up shocked to find his door ajar. Chance stood back and pulled his firearm from his side. Chance pushed open the front door and stepped in, gun drawn. The living room was empty and Chance stepped lightly on the wood floor, careful not to make any sound. Making his way toward the kitchen, he poked his head through the doorway. Nobody was inside, but Chance noticed that one of the kitchen knives was missing from the knife block that he kept on the counter. Chance turned and moved down the hall toward the backroom, clearing closets and the bathroom as he went. As moved closer to his bedroom, Chance could see light coming from under the door. Chance put his shoulder up to the door, turned the knob, and threw open the door!

Aryn screamed, surprised at the sudden appearance of Chance with his gun drawn. In her hands, she held the knife from the kitchen and what looked like a plate of cheese. On the dresser was a glass of red wine. "How did you get in?" Chance demanded, quickly getting over the initial shock of seeing her.

Aryn took a deep breath to compose herself and then explained. "I came back this morning to talk to you, but by the time I made it here, you had already left. I knocked for a while, thinking you might still be in bed. The landlord heard me and, thankfully, let me in. I just wanted you to know I decided not to run the story that we talked about last night, I didn't think it was right considering…"

Chance holstered his pistol but kept silent, waiting for the whole story.

Aryn lowered herself onto the bed and began again. "Anyways, I felt bad about leaving you the way I did, so I just hung out here until you came back. I see now that this was a mistake. I'm sorry." Aryn's big eyes filled with tears, and she looked down at her lap. Chance walked toward her; he was a sucker for a crying woman, always had been. He leaned down and cupped her face gently with his hands, drawing her up to look at him.

"It's okay, Aryn. I'm just glad I get to see you again," Chance assured her as he wiped away a tear with his thumb. He gently kissed her lips and pulled her toward him.

Aryn smiled and threw her arms around him. "You didn't think I would just leave after last night, did you?" she said in a playful whisper.

It was Chance's turn to smile. "Not even for a minute!"

Chapter 6

Murder Most Foul

Rain began to fall from the ominous dark gray clouds that overhung the city. Casting their dark shadows across the oil-stained streets that weaved their way through the surrounding buildings like a maze. Charlie smiled and leaned forward in his chair to get a better look from the Starbucks window. Something about the rain soothed him. It seemed to wash away the constant anger that plagued his conscience. All around him, he could sense the depression that fell with the rain weighing down everyone's mood. Charlie pondered why that would make him so delighted for a few minutes. It might be because the rain seemed to make everyone else as unhappy as he was the rest of the time. Or perhaps it was that it made people a bit more docile, a little more acceptable to be around. Took the edge off, if you will.

Charlie looked about him, admiring the quiet little room that was filled with the different fragrances that one associates with different teas and coffees from around the world. He pulled his coffee toward him and wrapped his hands around the hot mug. Years of working at a factory had left his hands aching all the time, so he gladly let the warmth ebb into his tired hands.

He had been going to this same shop, faithfully, for over fifteen years. Even before it was a Starbucks. The baristas had come to know his ritualistic order. Black coffee, no sugar, no cream. The first few times he had come in, they tried, in vain, to get him to order by using the names on the menu. But Charlie became overly annoyed about using words like *Grande* and *Blonde Roast Coffee*, so they eventually gave up and greeted him with his mug and a smile. Charlie appreciated their attempts to culture him but knew he was beyond changing. As a matter of fact, the only person that had ever been able to really make any changes in his life was his fiancée, Tammy. He sat there silently reflecting on the previous night. She had left for work, like usual, but when it came to her usual time to come home, she never did. He tried to call, worried that something had happened, but his calls were ignored and eventually just sent to voicemail. Eventually, around 4:00 a.m., she stumbled into the house, drunk from a night out at a bar. This wasn't like her. He reprimanded her for not letting him know where she was or even if she was safe. It wasn't about her going out. He knew everyone needed nights like that occasionally; it was a courtesy thing.

Breathing in deep, he let a small frown creep to the corners of his lips. Drawing himself back to the present, he looked about the room. All the usual people were there, slaves to caffeine, everything fell back into place. Except for one person. The manager had a young trainee in tow. They made their way around the room, stopping at different tables taking orders. Being that it was the trainee's first day, it took her a while to get all the orders written down. It took at least ten minutes for her and the manager to make it to his table.

"Good morning, sir! What can I get for you today?" the young woman asked him in a forced jovial tone.

Looking down at his now empty mug, Charlie ordered. "Black coffee, no sugar, no cream."

The young woman seemed relieved. But as she turned back toward her manager, she noticed her scowl. Quickly, she turned around. "Indivisible Blend, House Blend, or Café Verona?" she asked, looking up at the ceiling, trying to remember her unending list of flavored coffees.

Chance sat back and pondered this. In truth, he never knew what he was getting. It was always just black and strong. Normally, he would be annoyed, but something made him want to order it correctly today. Unsure of just why that was, he looked confused. The manager grimaced and came to the girl's rescue. "We know what he wants," she told her and smiled at him.

Charlie watched as she led the girl back to the register. Charlie was suddenly aware he was embarrassed that he didn't even know what kind of coffee he drank. He knew that it was something about the trainee. Charlie swallowed hard and walked to the front register to try and redeem himself. "Yes, sir, what can I get you?" the girl asked with the same forced smile.

Charlie looked around, desperate to find a coffee name that he could claim he drank. The silence must have been noticed by the manager because she pointed to Café Verona on the menu. He smiled at her gratefully and said the name of the coffee. The girl gave him a confused look but added a note to her order book. He turned away quickly to hide his face turning to a deep shade of red and marched back to his table. The manager brought over his coffee and sat down. Charlie didn't acknowledge her at first but couldn't ignore her long because he felt her eyes burning holes in what felt like his forehead. Charlie looked up and managed a smile. "Thanks for the help back there."

She smiled smugly and asked. "You have been coming here for seven years and never once bothered to learn the type of coffee you drink. Why today?" But she didn't need a response, she knew. Charlie looked away embarrassed and stared out the window.

The manager nodded and got up from the table. But before she walked away, she looked back and said, "Her name is Tina." He stayed there for several hours hurrying through his coffee so Tina would come back and speak with him. He even let her talk him into different flavors of coffee. He would try and choke some back and then smile like he had enjoyed every drop. It was worth it, just to see her smile.

She was a talker. Charlie liked that most about her; it helped fill in the voids of his silence. After just a few short conversations, it became so they could almost tell what the other person was thinking, without them voicing it. This, as you can imagine, worried Chance on a very personal level. But it didn't matter to him. He was in love, unfortunately, with two very different women.

After he couldn't stand to drink another bitter drop, Charlie smiled, said his goodbyes, and headed for the door. Charlie had a lot of ground to cover today. In his last letter, he promised to find the individual responsible for all the prostitutes' deaths as of late. And someone had decided that they were going to be his personal marshal in the local paper yesterday. It wasn't that he minded what they said. It was just that he was surprised that the police were basically broadcasting that they didn't already have the situation in hand. He had always thought that he and the police were just playing a drawn-out game of chess. But this seemed like something out of the Old West. The paper didn't say who was quoted yesterday, but it was obvious to Charlie. It sounded like the boisterous cop that had insulted him in the paper just a few days ago. Charlie would have to deal with him sooner or later, but for now, the fact that another predator was hunting in his area weighed heavier on his mind.

The police had just recently started tying these murders together. But he had been watching in fascination as this new pawn with a bloodlust raged through different cities. Leaving a wake of bodies behind like a tornado. Some people had an artistic eye for sculpture and others for oil paintings, but Charlie could see the beauty in every brutal stroke of a knife. And this new person was a budding master. Each prostitute was strangled with what seemed like a piano wire and carefully laid on their backs. Not to display but rather to rest. Their eyes were closed to hide the last few moments of horror that would forever be locked in place. Eyes don't just naturally close this way after someone dies; they have to be purposely closed. This meant the killer had even spent time after each to gently massage the rigor mortis out of the young women's cheeks and jawline to give them the appearance of sleeping peacefully, all while ensuring there wouldn't be any fingerprints on the skin. What was even more impressive was the fact that nothing was taken from them after they had passed. Most serial murderers took a trophy. Something to look back on fondly in their rest periods. Most people would take a tooth or even a vital organ with them. He had read about a man who actually scalped his victims alive. But this was something different. At every crime scene, there was a gift. A token of appreciation if you will. And it wasn't because of some sort of sex act. The killer had never slept with any of them. This was like he adored them. Worshipped them in some way. At some locations, he had left a locket or necklace; at others, just a flower. But one thing remained constant at all the murder scenes. A photo of them with a different facial feature cut out. It seemed odd to Charlie. Why would you cut out a piece of a photo and not the entire individual? Perhaps it was a particular feature the victim possessed that the killer treasured, and yet it still made little sense.

If this new killer had stayed out of his city, then this wouldn't be an issue. Like most predators, serial killers are extremely territorial. Like wolves, they marked their hunting grounds. The dominant wolf marks their hunting areas with urine scent, a warning to visiting wolves. A killer marks his with newspaper headlines, and Charlie was the Alpha in this city. This new blood had knowingly challenged him for territorial rights. As much as Charlie despised people in general, he had become somewhat fond of Dayton's citizens. Charlie had been contemplating taking care of this challenge himself when he was accused of committing the prostitute murders. Charlie seethed inside. He had worked so hard to explain his side of the killings. Each one had deserved it! But this? This was nothing like him. All of the carefully written explanations to the police had been for nothing! He could see then that the only way for the police to understand the difference between what he did and other killers was to help them catch this new blood. Knocking out two birds with one stone.

Today he was going to the last stigmatized property to see if he could find something the police had missed. By the time he finally arrived at the warehouse, it was deserted. Just a few police tape lines still hung from the busted windows, fluttering in the wind. Charlie, careful not to attract attention, stepped into the dark interior. It had been several days since the police had found the body, strangled with piano wire, but the stench of death still hung in the air. Charlie looked carefully around at the floor. The investigating detectives had scarred what visible prints may have laid in the dust with their own. The only thing that remained was the bloodstain that lay in the center of the room. He cautiously stepped around the bleached red spot, careful not to disturb the chalk outline in the center. Even the white line that surrounded the body of the prostitute showed the care in which she was displayed. With no arms represented, it was obvious that she had them folded across her chest or abdomen like she was asleep. He stood up slowly, scanning the closest wall. Something about them seemed out of place. It was nothing that was too obvious. It was painted the same dull gray that the rest were, but still... Charlie took a few steps in its direction to get a closer look. Some hoodlum, probably in hopes of impressing his friends, had scribbled out his "thug" name in large letters across the wall. Maintenance workers had then painted over it but it still left the form of the letters behind it. Charlie rolled his eyes. How was it that these kids had no money for college or saving for a car but had the money for several different colors of paint to tag the city in? Charlie was just turning away when he noticed a small arrow pointing down from the corner of the last letter. He hesitated and spun toward the wall again. The arrow itself was just a shade different from the rest of the gray paint. The paint had run a little bit. This was not the work of the original painter. Of course, the arrow could mean nothing. Just something meaningless, perhaps a marking for building purposes or even remnants of a previous tag that had been painted over by a rival gang member. And being its size, Charlie could easily see why the police would pay it no attention.

Charlie walked to the base of the wall just below the arrow and scanned the dust around him. *Strange*, he thought. *Nothing seems to be disturbed.* He backed a few steps away from the wall confused. If it was left there by the individual responsible for the young lady's death, then there should have been a clue or something. Charlie mulled over the meaning and finally gave up and turned to leave. Suddenly, a voice rang out. "Stop where you are, place your hands on your head, and turn slowly around!"

Charlie, a sociopath at heart, didn't even blink twice when surprised. He placed his hands in the air and took his time turning around, using that brief moment to work up a cover story.

Chapter 7

The Meeting

Gershing, pleased with himself, pointed his weapon at the man's back. "I'm not going to say it again! Place your hands on your head and turn around!" He demanded once more. The man raised his hands and slowly turned to face him. His face was an emotionless mask as he complied with Gershing's demands. "What are you doing here?" the excited detective asked.

"I'm sorry, Detective. I should have called ahead first. I'm with the FBI task force that was assigned to the Charlie case, just arrived from Cincinnati. Now we are waiting for the rest of the team," the man said as his mouth formed a smooth smile.

Gershing lowered his weapon in disgust. "Damn it. I thought you were another reporter," he said as he holstered the Glock. "They have been a real problem."

The man nodded and lowered his hands and brushed his hair away from his forehead. "Yeah, I can imagine," he said casually and walked toward Gershing. "I'm Agent Prater, Cincinnati branch. I didn't catch your name?" He reached into his jacket.

Gershing assumed it was to get his credentials out. Gershing was deadly wrong. He hadn't even finished uttering "Gershin..." before his body dropped to the floor. Confused, he tried to sit up but found he couldn't move. Frantic, he struggled with everything he had to make sense of what was happening. Through slowly closing eyes, he saw the so-called agent standing over him with the same fake smile he had used earlier. In his hand was an oddly shaped gun.

Charlie watched the detective's eyes close with smug satisfaction. Placing the dart gun back in his jacket, he bent over and checked to make sure the man was still breathing. It was a particularly strong anesthesia, meant for sedating bears. "Amazing what you can find on the internet," Charlie explained, needlessly, to the already unconscious officer. It wouldn't do to end this game too quickly. He grabbed Gershing by the belt and hoisted his massive frame up and over his shoulder. Charlie marched swiftly toward the door then stopped suddenly. "What was below that arrow?" He dropped Gershing unceremoniously and turned back toward the wall. He again looked for any signs that the ground had been disturbed. Finding nothing, he began to grow restless. It wouldn't be long before somebody else came here, being an active crime scene. Charlie pulled out a nitrile glove from his pocket and placed it on his non-dominant hand. This would allow him to leave no prints on the wall. He stuck his finger into the dust and then wrote a word onto the blue spray paint. Stepping back to admire his work. He smiled and turned to grab the unconscious detective. His footsteps faded quietly as he walked away into the darkened warehouse toward a swift escape.

Hours later, he placed his pen to paper and wrote another letter. Finishing, Charlie reread the short note and, satisfied, placed it in an envelope and grabbed a knife off the counter. Gershing's muffled demands down the dark hallway were cut to a gurgled scream. After a labored several minutes, Charlie stood back to admire his work. Satisfied, he dragged what remained of Gershing back down the hallway.

*****

Hello, from your friendly neighborhood psychopath:

I feel like I should explain my actions earlier today. I didn't kill that girl. However, I can't sit here and say for certain that I am free of guilt. Another wolf has started hunting. You know; I can't help but feel that if a certain somebody had shut their mouths instead of blabbing all over the news about me, just to make a name for themselves, then this wouldn't have happened. As to that…I will take care of him. Can't have him running his mouth again.

Oh, and not sure if you got my message at the warehouse? It was pretty pointed. I like the way we had it before Detective Ronings. Just you and I. I watched your date last night. She's beautiful. Hold her close detective. Cherish her. Well, I will leave you with this.

"I was born with the devil in me. I could not help the fact that I was a murderer, no more than the poet can help the inspiration to sing—I was born with the 'Evil One' standing as my sponsor beside the bed where I was ushered into the world, and he has been with me since."

Do you know who said that? H. H. Holmes.

Truly an inspiration.

Well, I have some weight to shed,
Charlie

Chapter 8

The Perfect Cast

Halfway across town, Chance was fighting the urge to answer the ringing phone on his nightstand. Aryn groaned and drew her arm from his chest. "Go ahead…" she muttered and half-smiled.

Chance made his apologies and pressed the screen to answer. "Detective Ronings."

Chance listened intently, his eyes concerned. "All right, I'll head back to the cop shop." Chance sat up and grabbed his gun off the nightstand. "I have to head back. One of our officers never checked back in last night." Aryn nodded and started to get up. "No, it's okay, you can stay as long as you want."

Aryn blushed and smiled. "I don't know if we are quite on that level yet."

He shrugged. "I can't think of anyone else I would rather have stayed here." Still smiling, she pulled on his long sleeve shirt and headed toward the kitchen. Chance watched her hips sway and sighed. *Gershing better be dead*, he thought sarcastically. Chance stood to get dressed and hurried out the door. Passing Aryn in the kitchen, he paused just long enough to kiss her on the forehead while straightening his tie. "I'll see you tonight?" Aryn grinned and nodded. He reached for the door handle, smiling, and pulled it closed behind him.

Love has been around since literally the beginning of time, but Chance felt this was special. Different from everyone else's experience. A chemical reaction, yes, but also something spiritual. Of course, he was wrong, but to him, like all of us, it seemed unique. He would have skipped to his car if he hadn't conditioned himself his entire adult life to appear manly or strong. He grounded his feet and walked casually toward his car. He didn't often drive from his apartment, but the urgency of the captain's call warranted it. Still reeling from her kiss, he drove toward the precinct, his mind only on her. The ten-minute drive to work was haunted by her scent, her presence, and her soulful eyes. Lust in its purest form.

Chance pulled into the security lot and parked his car. He sat for a moment, reluctant to go into the office. Taking a deep breath, he shut off his engine and opened the door. The office was abuzz with people in all types of uniforms using radios and phones trying desperately to get a hold of Gershing. He quickened his pace and knocked on the captain's door. Rashan called him in and waved at an open seat.

Tom and Turtle were already sitting. Chance nodded a solemn greeting, sat, and waited for Rashan to speak. "Gershing never reported back in after his shift last night. His weapon is still signed out of the armory." The captain shook his head and caught his breath before continuing. "We turned on the transponder in his car, and I sent two officers over to check it out. While that's all pissing me off, it still isn't the bad part! His car is outside of the warehouse where they found the last victim. Which makes it your case." Tom swore under his breath and leaned over, resting his elbows onto his knees. Turtle leaned back and raised his hands onto his head. Chance stared at the captain, trying to make sense of what was happening. Questions swirled around his mind. What was he doing there? What does this mean? Where is that dumbass? Only the first question seemed to have an obvious answer. Gershing had never been able to stay out of the limelight. A glory hound ever since Chance had met him. He was trying to solve this case on his own.

"So what's our next move?" Chance asked.

The captain shrugged and remained silent.

Chance nodded and stood up. "Well, it's still our case, so I'm headed over there. Tom, Turtle, you guys want to come along?"

Tom took a deep breath and stood to follow. Turtle nodded but remained sitting to ask one more question. "If we find him…if we find him, but he's not in a condition to be brought back, what do you want us to do?"

The captain stared back, confused.

"What the hell do you mean?" the captain replied angrily.

Turtle stood and smoothed his suit top before continuing. "Well, I mean serial killers often revisit the scene of the crime. It gives them a sort of sexual thrill. There is a good chance that he bumped into him last night. And if that is the case, announcing it to the media could only fuel Charlie's passion. It's never good to continue to feed into the legend they have built in their own mind." Turtle finished the sentence in almost a calming whisper.

The captain sat back with his hands resting flat on the desk and thought about it for a minute before answering. "Do what you think is best. But find him. He may have been an asshole, but he was our asshole." Chance opened the door and headed down the hall with the FBI in tow.

It was a long ride toward the center of Dayton. Traffic was at its highest in the morning. Backed up for miles with people inching their way closer to work. It was a silent but anxious ride. Tom stared out the passenger side window, and Turtle had buried his face in his laptop. Chance stared straight ahead, struggling not to flip on his lights. He knew it wouldn't do any good with traffic being as bad as it was. On the surface, he hoped to find Gershing somewhere at a bar nearby passed out. But deep down, he had a sinking feeling that he wouldn't find him alive. Traffic slowly sped up just past the first few exits. That's where most of the businesses had set up, along the river.

Chance took the exit toward the warehouse. Passing the Children's Hospital, he slowed to let a mother push a stroller across the street. Tom looked at the pair and sighed, shaking his head. "It's crazy that life just keeps shuffling on like there isn't a psycho walking among them waiting to kill one of them."

Chance nodded and started driving again. "You know, I have been chasing these animals for what seems like forever, and they all seemed the same. Until now. This one doesn't have a purpose. No

Modus Operandi. He is just killing whoever pisses him off that day. Like he's Batman or something. It's nuts!" he grumbled, throwing his fist into the ceiling of the car.

Turtle looked up from his laptop. "Calm down, Tom." Chance didn't know how to answer. He didn't even understand why Charlie had chosen him of all people to contact.

Two squad cars were already parked outside when they finally pulled into the adjacent lot. Turtle closed the screen on the computer and placed it back inside of his backpack before getting out to follow the other two into the building. As they stepped in, the building was dark. Chance searched on the wall for a light switch to no avail. Turtle allowed the door to swing shut, making a loud clang, lending to the ominous aura. Chance shrugged off a nervous shudder that ran from his lower back all the way up to his shoulders, and Tom called out to the other officers that were sent out to find Gershing. With no answer, they turned on their flashlights, drew their weapons, and continued down the long hallway toward the main warehouse. Not a word was shared between the trio, but they all shared the same thought. This place felt off, like just before a storm. Suddenly, Chance's light fell upon the two officers crumpled in a heap just outside the large double doors that separated the entrance to the main part of the building! Quickly, the three bent to check for life signs. The two men were breathing and had slow strong pulses, almost as if they were sleeping. Chance reached for the radio on one of the officers and reported the condition of the two. Turtle stayed back to guard the two men and try to revive them. As Chance and Tom stood, they approached the door cautiously. Whatever had attacked the two men might still be in the area. Chance knew from experience that a trapped animal was at its most dangerous when it was cornered, and he wasn't going to take any chances.

Tom leaned against the side of the door and nodded for Chance to go through, indicating that he had his back. Chance pushed the door open with his knee and entered one hand on his flashlight and his other resting atop of the other with his pistol at the ready should there be a need to pull the trigger. A bead of sweat dripped from his forehead and landed on his nose. The room was pitch black. Tom swung in behind him and touched his shoulder. Chance looked back as Tom indicated the light switch on the wall. Chance nodded his approval, and Tom reached back and flipped the switch. The light flooded the room, temporarily blinding the two men. As their eyes came accustomed to the light, a horrific sight came into focus. There, in the center of the large floor, laid a bloody, misshapen Gershing!

Chance holstered his weapon and ran to him. Tom followed, gun still pointing this way and that to ensure that there was no danger still lying in wait. Chance slid to a stop and dropped beside the man. He placed two fingers on the man's throat, desperately trying to find a pulse. After what seemed like an eternity, there was one weak beat and then another. Chance bent his head to listen to Gershing's breathing. It was weak and labored. Tom called all clear and leaned over to help Chance. Gershing's head was wrapped in a bandage of sorts, as were his hands.

Chance stood and reached for his cell phone. After a tense phone conversation, he hung up and bent back down. "All right, the ambulance is on the way."

Tom nodded. "Check this out," he almost whispered, his face pale. He reached down and gingerly lifted the bandage from Gershing's face. Where his eyes used to rest, there were just two bloody empty sockets. Gershing moaned, and his jaw opened, allowing a small stream of blood to dribble down his chin. Chance swallowed hard and pointed his flashlight into the void. The man's tongue no longer would aid him in talking. It had been cut cleanly out.

Tom turned away, sickened to his stomach. "Damn it! Who in the…?" Chance turned Gershing's head to the side to keep him from drowning in his own blood. Sirens wailed closer from outside, giving notice to the two men that help was on its way. A few minutes passed as Chance and Tom tried to make what was left of Gershing comfortable. They may not have liked the man, but no one deserved this level of butchering. It took a cold heart to do this sort of thing.

The muffled sounds of the paramedics came from behind the double doors. Chance laid his hand on Gershing, trying to reassure him that help was on the way. As the rescue team ran in with the gurney, the two men stood back to give them room. Tom stayed there quietly for a moment and then turned away. Chance took a deep breath and followed. His head was still reeling from what he had just witnessed. The two spent the next hour, sweeping the room for clues to no avail. Disappointed, they headed back to their car to find Turtle sitting on the hood with his laptop on his lap. "Hey! Did you guys find anything?" he asked. Chance shook his head and leaned against the side of the car, burying his head in his hands. Tom explained what had happened as Turtle ran his fingers furiously across the keyboard, writing a report for later reference. As the two conversed, a uniformed officer approached. "Detective?" he asked, trying to get Chance's attention. Nodding at the two agents, he continued only after Chance acknowledged him. "They just got Gershing to the hospital and the other officers are recovering well. Also, we have a team sweeping the area and brushing for prints but nothing yet."

Chance nodded and said, "Thanks. Do your best, okay? This was one of our own."

The officer dropped his head under the gravity of the situation. "Yeah... How could anyone do this? I mean the bastard even shoved something into his ears and busted his eardrums. He will never hear again!" Chance's eyes sparked, and his heart raced. In all of the blood-soaked bandages on his face, he had overlooked the blood on the side of his ears, assuming that it was from the eyes.

Turtle looked up from his keyboard and said excitedly, "Holy crap! That's the whole package! Hear no evil, speak no evil, and see no evil!"

Tom and Chance's eyes met across the roof of the car. He had left Gershing no way to let us know who had done this to him! "That's not good... I didn't think it was important at the time, but his hands were crushed with what looks like a hammer of some sort. It will be a while before he can even write. If ever!" the officer said. Chance slammed his fist into the side of the car, furious with the situation. After a few minutes, he raised his head and looked out over the horizon. Gem city had never looked so gray.

A short while later, they found themselves driving silently back to the station. In fact, not a word was spoken the entire trip. Chance used this time to collect his thoughts. Had Charlie done this? Or had a completely different person? Gershing must have seen him. Was there any way for him to convey what he had seen? Even a simple description would be enough to know they were on the right track. It was infuriating. How could anyone have even got the drop on Gershing? The fact was, there were a hundred questions and, so far, no answers. He turned into the parking lot, and the three men headed into the building to find the captain.

Rashan was hurriedly moving stacks of paper this way and that across his desk, all while holding the phone against his shoulder with his ear. He would yell into the receiver occasionally and then listen intently, waiting for his turn again. The men stood in front of the massive mahogany desk, waiting for the captain to have the time to get their report. After a few minutes, the captain slammed the phone back into its charger and took a deep breath before beginning. "Okay… Are you guys all right?" The men nodded. Relieved, he continued. "Gershing is in stable condition, down at Good Sam. It looks like he will make it. Damn it! God! How could this happen?" Knowing he wouldn't get an answer from the three, he drummed his fingers on his desk and then began again. "Well… I don't know. I'm at a loss for words right now. Did you guys find anything?" Charlie answered that he hadn't and that they were hoping that forensics would find something. "Nothing yet. But they're still scrubbing the scene. The hospital did find a note inside one of his shirt pockets. They are faxing it over now." Rashan informed them. The men began describing the events in vivid detail to the captain. Just as it came time for Tom to tell his narrative the fax machine purred to life. Each man fell silent in nervous anticipation and hopes that what came across the printer would lead to some sort of clue. They were not to be disappointed. The captain walked to the tray and began reading. He stopped to reread it again and handed it to Chance. It was a letter from Charlie.

Chapter 9

Now Reel It In...

Charlie thumbed through the pages of the paper, searching for any news of the other killer. Nothing yet. He was obviously biding his time till he could best get his attention. But he was wrong, Charlie was all ears now. He closed the paper and laid it neatly on the table before him. Lifting a cup of warm coffee to his mouth, he took a long swallow and leaned back into the chair to think. It would only be a matter of time before his rival would kill again. Killers are not hobbyists; they don't just do it because they want to. They need it. Like smokers need nicotine. It drives them, leaves them wanting more. The rule of three... At least that's what the FBI believed. This was the first, two more to go. Then there would be a resting period. But that wasn't necessarily the case. Son of Sam didn't have a resting period, and neither did H. H. Holmes. They just continued until they were caught. Hell, at his height, Holmes was believed to have killed hundreds of innocents. Was he any different? Charlie took a deep breath and reassured himself that he was. He only did it because it needed to be done. He had never killed an innocent. Everybody had deserved it in some way. Gershing was no exception. He had planted evidence, mistreated suspects; he had even boldface lied to get himself into the position he was currently in. Charlie had killed for a lot less. *People shouldn't be so rude...* Charlie lamented. He needed a new perspective. He closed his eyes, leaned back in his chair, and stretched his arms, resting them behind his head. Charlie knew that this was personally directed at him. It might be his ego, but he truly felt like this was a calling out of sorts. Like lions in a pride, he was being challenged for territory. Honestly, it was infuriating. But Charlie couldn't fall into the anger; it would make him sloppy, and he needed to be at the top of his game to play both sides of the fence. If he was searching for a new target, who would it be? Perhaps he needed to actually find one. Sometimes the best hunters don't search for the animal; they find the prey. Charlie smiled and opened his eyes. He knew just where to start…

He folded his newspaper in half, tucked it under his arm, and headed for the door. It would take him about twenty minutes to get where he was going by car if the traffic wasn't too bad. Around four o'clock, people started heading home from their mundane workday, and with Dayton installing traffic lights pretty much every two hundred feet, traffic could get pretty backed up. If he hurried, he could beat the clock. Before leaving he looked back and waved goodbye to Tammy. Waving back, she shot him a quick smile and blew him a kiss. Charlie grinned and bent his head down. He wasn't used to love. In truth, he had always found it to be distracting, and in his line of work that could cause a slip-up. His ignition roared to life, and he was on his way. Checking his mirrors, he pulled onto the street and headed down the hill toward Chance's house. Chance would of course be at work, puzzling over Charlie's last letter. Imagining all the pandemonium going on right now in the precinct made Charlie smile. It wasn't that he enjoyed screwing with the police; it was that it served as a distraction for whatever served him at the moment. Carefully crafting each note to misdirect people away from the truth. And they always bought into it. Charlie thought that perhaps they took it as God's word because they couldn't imagine someone being a killer and a liar at the same time. Honestly, he didn't know for sure. Chance managed to cut five minutes off the trip by cutting through a neighborhood and pulling in behind Chance's apartment. Positioning himself just out of view behind a tree, he settled in to watch for Aryn.

Aryn was the best logical choice to get Charlie's rival's attention. Charlie realized that by pointedly addressing Chance, he had made him a target. While Charlie had grown to respect the detective, it wasn't why he originally wrote to him. If Charlie had the ability to feel any sympathy, he would feel awful. For the time being, the best thing he could do was follow Aryn in hopes that she would lead him to his target. Charlie watched her through the window as she busied herself around the kitchen. Scurrying around grabbing this and that to, what appeared, make dinner. Charlie let his mind drift for a moment, imagining Tammy doing the same thing at home. Charlie truly enjoyed watching her cook. The way she would battle with her long layers swinging in front of her eyes as she stirred this and that, she honestly never looked more beautiful to him. Shaking himself back into reality, he concentrated on the task at hand. Drifting off could be extremely dangerous for everybody. Aryn stopped what she was doing and turned her eyes toward the front door. The light level changed slightly in the kitchen, indicating the front door had just opened and closed. Judging by the amount of time the light changed, it appeared that the door was casually opened, meaning the person who came in belonged there. If it had only flickered for an instant, then somebody would have been in a hurry to get out of view from the street. Charlie watched Aryn through the window, waving happily at whoever came in. Chance drew into view and wrapped his arms around her, pulling her in for a firm kiss. They held each other and smiled. Then Chance drew away, removed his sports jacket, and headed out of sight toward what Charlie assumed was the bedroom. Aryn leaned against the counter and crossed her arms. Charlie sighed and started the car. If Aryn was the target, then his adversary wouldn't waste their time doing something if Chance was home. Too risky. Being that the street was clear, it was a safe bet that they weren't being watched by anyone at the moment. He buckled his seatbelt and pulled away. Perhaps it was time to use Aryn as the bait she had made herself. It would take some planning, but with some thought on the matter, he believed he might ensure his rival sped things up. After all, he couldn't spend every minute of his day following her around.

Twenty minutes later, Charlie pulled into his driveway and headed into the house. The house was a beautiful washed brick ranch in Centerville. The shutters needed some work, but he hadn't found the time to paint the new ones he had purchased to replace them. He shrugged his shoulders, thinking of the pain it was going to be, and pushed open his door. The scent of roast filled his nostrils, and he inhaled deeply. Memories of his mother's cooking flooded over him, remembering the few happy memories that came with that. Smiling, he headed to the kitchen to take Tammy in his arms. She hugged him lightly back and then drew away too busy herself with what appeared to be gravy. It seemed like a strained hug. It had been that way lately. Charlie chalked it up to stress but lamented on watching Chance and Aryn. It seemed so genuine and natural.

"How was your day?" Tammy asked with her back still turned.

"Pretty good. Yours?"

She turned and wiped her bangs away from her face. "Busy," she said and took a breath before continuing. "I swear people just come to the shop to order the fanciest food to seem refined for their friends." She rolled her eyes and turned back to grab the bowl of gravy from the counter.

Charlie shook his head smiling. "I noticed that. I don't know why people do that. Probably the same reason they sit all day at coffee shops and pretend to be writing a book." She shrugged her shoulders and agreed. They sat down to dinner and casually talked about each other's days. He carefully avoided mentioning his excursion to Chance's house, instead centered on his office work and the lame jokes he had heard throughout his day. She politely chuckled occasionally and then listed all of the ways she had intentionally misspelled customers' names on their cups.

Tammy, while never knowing that she slept by a monster every night, had still grown weary of him. Charlie had been keeping up appearances for a while, but his cold heart had shown through. His dead eyes now seemed hollow and unfriendly, completely different from how he felt for her, but it wasn't enough. Years of the deadpan eyes had broken her spirit, leaving a shadow of whom she used to be. He couldn't change his eyes even if he tried, and on some level, she knew that, and still she had grown weary. On top of that, he was still a man, and like most men, Charlie naturally had a hard time showing their affection, combined with the gnawing suspicion he was hiding something from her, had created something she had little interest in.

They finished dinner and then joined each other on the front porch to talk. Charlie sat on the bench thinking that she would sit beside him, but instead, she sat in the separate chair to the left. His eyes dropped in disappointment, but he forced a smile on his face anyways. She silently stared out into the sky at the shrinking light, appreciating the sunset creeping through the breaks in the clouds. She could feel moisture building and knew there was a storm growing. Charlie chattered about this and that throughout his day, and she nodded occasionally, wrapped up in her own thoughts. She had felt so empty over the last few months, and it had grown hard to even listen to him. It was true that she loved him, but it wasn't the same as when they had first met. She struggled to remember the excitement she felt when they first touched or first pressed their lips together passionately. It saddened and embittered her in the same moment. But she continued trying to come back to Charlie; unfortunately, it seemed like the more she tried, the more she was pushing herself away. Charlie watched her frown and asked what was wrong. She shrugged her shoulders, uncommitted, and said nothing. Charlie nodded and watched her drift back off to her own thoughts.

"Are you going back out tonight?" he asked. It bothered him that she was going out drinking that much, but when he voiced his disapproval, she would get mad and it seemed to make things worse. Charlie was stuck up a creek without a paddle and didn't know what to do.

"Yeah. Just for a little bit," she answered after an awkward silence. He nodded and folded his arms across his chest. He missed her desperately and couldn't stand the distance that had grown between them. If he had a heart to break, it would be in pieces on the floor. Instead, it was just making him irritated. Actually, it was the most anger he had ever experienced. It wasn't the type of anger that rises when somebody wrongs you; it was the kind that could only evolve in a dark well of desperation. The kind that welled up and overcame your senses, like drowning in an invisible wave. Suffocating, destructive, and life-shattering. He couldn't bring himself to forgive and yet couldn't let his love go for her. He would have horrible visions of her with other men. Waking up drenched in sweat desperately reaching out for her beside him in bed, only to find the cold impression left where she usually slept. It had been that way for a while. It flooded every pore of his being, both frightened and enraged him. The constant threat of her finding someone new quickly became too much for him to handle, almost to the point of following her on her nightly trips to the bar. But he never did. He didn't want to become the person she thought him to be. Controlling and jealous. Those were the adjectives that she often used during their arguments.

He tried to show her that he was different but was afraid it didn't matter anymore. Yet hope remained, probably a waste, but he still reached deeper and deeper each time she went out, never once inviting him, to find the patience and love that was still there. "I love you, Tammy," he said, meaning every syllable. She raised her eyes and looked at his impassioned face. She choked on the words for a moment, feeling even more at a loss. Like the last words she said to her dying mother, she wiped a bang from in front of her watery eyes. "I love you too."

He stood and stretched. If she was going out tonight, perhaps it was best that he used his time constructively. Aryn wasn't going to watch herself, and if he had the free time, then this was probably the best thing to do. Besides, it would keep his mind focused, which was something that he had been having trouble doing lately. He went inside saying nothing and started cleaning up the dishes. A few minutes went by until Tammy walked in, said goodbye, grabbed her keys off the counter, and walked out. Charlie walked to the window and watched her drive away into the approaching night. Confused, he wiped away a single tear from his eye and turned back to the task at hand.

He threw on a dark-gray hooded sweatshirt and headed for his car. Chance and Aryn would probably be finishing their dinner by now, and if he hurried, he could catch them just as they were settling in for the evening. He shuffled through the radio stations as he drove, trying to find a talk radio station that wasn't currently in the midst of a commercial break. His go-to station, WHIO, was currently pushing sales for a local flower shop. He was not in any mood to think about buying flowers for anyone but left it, hoping Clark Howard would come back on and continue his show. The man rattled endlessly about this sale and that sale at the flower shop, droning on and on. Charlie sighed and turned the radio down to a low mumble, continuing his drive this way until he pulled up behind Chance's apartment and settled in for the night to keep watch, hoping some sign of his rival would come. He leaned his seat back, turned back up the radio, and keenly scanned the area through his windshield. Clark Howard had begun his show again and was speaking about reverse mortgages. Charlie half-listened and turned his attention to the apartment window. It was hard to make out, but it looked like Aryn and Chance were watching television snuggled together on the couch in the living room. He could just make out the tops of their heads leaning together, but it was enough to know they were alive and well. Chance would occasionally pull his head away and reach for what Charlie assumed was his drink and then return in his original position. This went on for hours. Eventually, through the window, Charlie watched as Chance stood and headed down the hallway to his bedroom. The switch was thrown, and light flooded the room. Aryn waited a few moments and joined Chance, turning off lights as she went. A few moments later, the light went out as they joined each other in bed.

Charlie knew that if anything was going to happen this evening, it would be in the next few hours. Most crimes were committed by adults between the hours of 9:00 p.m. and 3:00 a.m. Being that it was already around 12:00 a.m., it was just a matter of time. Charlie sat up and paid closer attention to his surroundings. But for the next few hours, nothing happened. In fact, as the morning drew closer, it appeared that Charlie had misguessed the intended target. There should have been some sign by now. Perhaps someone else watching the apartment, but there was literally no movement from any other soul or car that night.

Charlie sighed and pulled away. He needed to get back before Tammy made it back from the bar. Plus a few hours of sleep would do him some good before he went to work. WHIO started back into its commercial break as he drove. Suddenly a new avenue of approach was given to Charlie, like a gift handed down from the heavens. Charlie finally had a way to bait the other killer. He smiled and reached for his phone.

Chapter 10

Charlie's Dilemma

Chance,

I need to apologize for leaving Gershing the way I did. The whole "See no evil, speak no evil, hear no evil" is extremely played out. Actually, it was more than that. Since I wasn't going to kill him just yet, I needed to make sure, as I would hope you already guessed, that he couldn't identify me later. Look, I don't feel like mincing words right now, so let me just say he deserved everything that happened to him. Not to mention if he had been where he was supposed to be that day, then he would still be walking and talking. Tony was a bad boy. He has been taking bribes all over the city since he joined the force. And that's just what I dragged out of him in the first hour of our time together. Anyways, I don't have a lot of time today. I have attached a confession, in his own words, to this. Enjoy.

PS. I wasn't joking before. Chance, you're too smart to be focusing just on me for all of the recent deaths. Start paying attention. Oh, and congratulations on the new girlfriend. She seems like a real keeper.

Charlie

I, Tony M. Gershing, have the following to unburden myself with.

When I was seventeen, I raped my girlfriend. She wasn't ready and I was mad about it, so I made her have sex with me. It was in her parents' basement, and she cried the whole time. When I was nineteen, I drugged a girl in college and had sex with her behind a dumpster. I cheated on my entrance exams into the Police Academy off a Mexican kid and then accused him of cheating off of me, resulting in him being permanently barred from joining the police training. I then cheated again on my detective exams. I am so sorry for everything.

Tony

Chance reread the letter, stifling the vomit rising up in his throat. Even if any of what Gershing had written was true, which Chance had a sneaking suspicion was, it just lent credence to what Charlie had done. If this were to get out, it would build a cult following. He swallowed hard and handed the letter to Tom the older of the two agents. Tom quietly read the letter and handed the ziplocked evidence bag it was in to Turtle. As Turtle was carefully going over the letter for any clues they may have missed, Tom spoke carefully. "This has to stay internal. If this gets out, we will be flooded with tips and fan letters from all over the country. We can't have that right now—it will just distract us from the evidence." Chance nodded and let his weary shoulders drop.

Captain Murphy sighed and rubbed his eyes. After a few moments, he spoke. "Okay, well, here's the problem. I have an entire precinct pissed off about an almost-cop killer, and if we don't catch this SOB. I can't promise they won't turn into a bunch of vigilantes."

Tom nodded. "I get that, but I am telling you I have been through this before. As soon as we tell anyone else, this gets leaked to the press, and we won't get this guy. Not to mention the fact that he is already killing outside of his usual MO with the hooker."

Turtle bounced his head up and down in agreement. "Yeah, the book is pretty clear on this one. We have to keep this in house and turn everything into headquarters for them to get forensics on this."

"Look, I get that, and we will, but we won't get any evidence to turn around anytime soon! And then what am I supposed to do in the meantime?" the captain argued, turning red in the face.

"Nothing," Turtle answered. "Charlie meets all of the signs of a sociopath with delusions of grandeur. If this gets out at all, it will only fuel his blood lust. The best thing we can do is keep this quiet for the time being, as best we can at least." The captain nodded sarcastically, threw his hands in the air, and began arguing the plan of action.

As Tom, Turtle, and the captain traded their heated discussion, Chance thought back on the letter. How did Charlie know about Aryn? Even as he asked himself that question, he knew it meant that they were being watched. It enraged and scared him at the same time. How long would it be until Charlie attacked Aryn or him? And even through all of this, something about the letter bothered him. The letter was very specific about the prostitute that was murdered. Charlie had thus owned every kill that he had made.

Chance interrupted the conversation sharply. "Why did Charlie say that I needed to start paying attention?"

Turtle and the captain fell silent, but Tom answered, "Look, these psychopaths always pick someone out to screw with. You're just the newest flavor of the month. Try and not to get too personally involved with these letters. It will compromise the investigation." Chance nodded but doubted him. He understood that between all of them Tom easily had the most experience. But something about this still bothered him. Even still, he tried to push his concerns out of his head and focus on the evidence.

Outside the captain's office, the precinct was abuzz with officers and detectives working together to get as much information and evidence they could about Gershing's attacker. Chance watched through the door at the hectic scene. It reminded him of a beehive when it was being attacked. Mindless drones buzzing about with no particular path, just set on one thing, protect the hive. Chance turned and waited patiently for the captain to quit speaking. "And that's why we are going to do it your way this time, but if this doesn't get something back in the next forty-eight hours, then we are doing it my way!" The captain loosened his tie from his reddening neck and took a breath. Tom rolled his eyes and said nothing.

"Is it possible this is what Charlie wants?" Chance asked. Tom looked confused but waited for Chance to finish. "I mean just look out there. We aren't going to get anything done with everybody in here scared and angry. What if he is doing this to distract from something else?"

Turtle stood and paced in front of the captain's desk. "It's possible. Hell, I don't know!" He was still hyped up from the argument that they were just in. He had been having a hard time separating his feelings from the case, probably due to his inexperience as an agent.

Tom watched his partner pace back and forth. He felt bad for him. This was a lot to put on a rookie, but unfortunately, the best agents were forged in fire, not in a classroom. And to top it all off, this was an especially difficult case. "What would he be distracting us from?" he asked. Chance shrugged his shoulders, defeated, and lowered his head into his hands, at a loss for an answer. Tom thought about this possibility for a minute. Was it possible it was something Charlie didn't want them to discover about an old murder, something they had missed? Or was it something he didn't want them to pay attention to now or in the future? It was even possible he was just screwing with them just to do it. There were so many possibilities it was overwhelming. But one thing was sure: it wasn't going to help just sitting around in here. Chance was definitely right about one thing. There was sheer pandemonium in the station. It was time to take charge and get the officers focusing their efforts, if they were ever going to catch Charlie. Tom turned to the captain to try and figure out a plan of action.

Twenty minutes later, the office door opened and Chance walked out. "Can I have your attention everyone?" he shouted over the roar of voices. Slowly, the noise died down as people stopped in their tracks and turned their heads toward the detective. "I know you are concerned about what happened to Detective Gershing. As of the moment, he is alive, although still in the ICU. This can be a frightening time, and I know many of you are angry. I promise you we will catch him! I have worked with a lot of competent officers during my time, and I want you to know I would never want to work with anyone better than you people here. You have proven yourselves loyal and dedicated officers of the law time and time again. We always get our man, and this time will be no different." Chance paused for a moment to let that sink in before beginning again. Everyone sat, letting the silence settle over them. The smell of burning coffee filled their nostrils.

"If we are going to get this done, we need to get some order around here. Detectives Williamson and Porter will be pulling some of you aside to assist them in their investigations by the end of the day. This team will be in charge of reinvestigating the past unsolved murders over the last ten years with the exception of the prostitute and Detective Gershing's attack. These will be being investigated by myself and the agents assisting us from the FBI—alone. Also, it has been decided that there will be a police detail assigned to protect Officer Gershing while he is in the hospital. Bravo traffic will be reassigned for this task as of now. Please head on over to the hospital and work out shifts amongst yourselves. This will be twenty-four-hour protection until further notice. The captain wants the Delta team to patrol Third Street over the next few nights at least. Round up all of the bridge girls and bring them in. We will interview them and press charges. We can get this guy, but we have to pull together!" Chance finished and turned back toward the captain's office, closing the door behind him. The officers looked around at each other for just a moment and then headed out to their new assignments.

As the door closed, Chance took his seat in front of Captain Murphy. Tom patted him on the back reassuringly and settled back into the leather armchair he was sitting in. "Good job, Detective," Murphy started. "That ought to bring things back to a more manageable level."

The old captain turned to Tom and gruffly added, "Send the letter off to your people and keep us in the loop. If we are to stand even a cold chance in hell of catching Charlie, then it's going to be because we worked openly with each other."

Tom nodded and grabbed the evidence bag with the letter off the captain's desk. "I'll get this off to headquarters today. Turtle will head over to your medical examiner and see what she got off of the prostitute and Gershing." Nodding to Turtle to ensure that Turtle understood his duties, he turned and left the office, closing the door softly behind him.

Turtle stood, awkwardly half-bowed, and walked out to see the medical examiner. But before leaving, he added, "I'll get back to you as soon as it's done. We will get him, guys, don't worry."

But Chance was worried. He still couldn't shake off how much Charlie knew about his personal life. The captain leaned back deeper into his chair and reached for a small desk drawer on his left. Pulling out two used Dixie cups and a bottle of cheap scotch, he poured and then offered Chance one. Chance, who rarely drank, reached out a shaking hand to grab it. They both took a long swallow on the bitter amber-colored alcohol. Chance winced a bit at the aftertaste. The captain smiled knowingly and let out a low chuckle. "When you have been doing this job as long as I have, you get used to swallowing bitter pills. Chance, I didn't want to say anything, but I think you're right to be worried about Charlie knowing about your lady friend. Go home and spend some time with her tonight. Just to be safe. I can't imagine Charlie being stupid enough to hang around if you're there too."

Chance silently agreed and went to stand.

"Before you go, swing by the hospital and see if the hospital has anything else off of Gershing. He may not be able to tell us who did this, but maybe something he had on him would help." Chance nodded and left.

After a quick call to Aryn to firm up a dinner date at his place that evening, he headed to his car to visit the hospital that was holding Gershing's belongings. It only took twenty minutes to get to Kettering Hospital so Chance didn't have long to sit with his thoughts as he drove. Was Charlie after him and Aryn, or was he just watching them? Either way, Chance was not comfortable. It was starting to make him paranoid. He kept checking his mirrors to see if he was being followed. Pulling up in front of the hospital, his memory was jogged to not long ago when he was there to have his appendix removed at this very hospital. It had been an extremely painful experience that had ended rather sadly, as no one had come and visited him in the hospital after the surgery. Chance frowned at the thought and parked his car. After checking the sign inside the door for directions to the Intensive Care Unit, he started a search for the stairs. Having the option between an elevator and stairs, he usually chose the latter. It just seemed like a healthier option. As he climbed the three flights of stairs, his thoughts drifted back to the letter.

Gershing had supposedly admitted to raping at least two girls when he was a young man. If this were true, it brought a whole new light on the situation. Just the thought of someone being raped was enough to make Chance's skin crawl. He had never dealt with the concept well. It was a disgusting crime, and it took away a lot from the victims. Their dignity, comfort with touch, and their sense of well-being are ripped from them, even ruining future relationships.

Chance shook his head and pushed open the door into the ICU's hallway. Walking up to the front desk, he pulled out his badge and explained why he was there. "Sure, I'll get that for you!" The bubbly nurse aide said, then asked if Chance wanted to visit Gershing. He started to say no and then felt guilty. He nodded. "Um, yeah." She smiled and led him into Gershing's room. She excused herself, saying that she would bring the evidence bags to him. He nodded and walked up to Gershing's bedside. The bruised and bloodied shell of a man before him was completely unrecognizable as the officer that Chance had known. Charlie had truly given him work over. Exposed in the gown that they had dressed him in, it became apparent that he had several chemical burns up and down his legs and arms. The red markings were still inflamed with skin peeling in long strips. The hospital had done their best at cleaning up what remained of the broken man, but it would be a long time before he looked like his old self, if he ever would. Plus being blinded and deaf, he would never be self-reliant in the same way again. He laid his hand onto Gershing's to let him know someone was there and heard a low gurgled moan escape the former detective. Chance instinctively withdrew his own hand. The young aide tapped him on the shoulder, scaring him. He jumped, turning toward her.

She smiled and said, "I'm sorry, I didn't mean to scare you! Here's the stuff you asked for. If you could just sign right here for it?" Chance smiled in return and signed the clipboard on the line she was pointing at.

"Thanks. Um, well, I guess, take good care of him," he said awkwardly. She nodded and assured him that they would. He took the bag of bloodied clothes and left, leaving the haunting reminder of Charlie's work behind him.

After swinging back by the office to drop off the evidence bag, he headed back to his apartment to meet Aryn for dinner. It was late afternoon when he pulled up in front and headed to the door. He pulled out his key, unlocked the door, and climbed the stairs to join Aryn in the kitchen. Aryn put down the spoon she had been stirring her pasta sauce with and met him at the top of the stairs. Chance wrapped her in his arms and kissed her hard on the mouth. He held her like this for a long moment, reveling in her touch. He could feel her warmth, her very essence as a woman. He pulled his head back and smiled. He couldn't ever remember being this happy.

Chapter 11

A Broken Heart Knows No Solace

Tammy raised her head from her steering wheel and looked through blurred eyes at Charlie's front door. How could she tell him? She had done the unthinkable. Something she didn't think she could ever do to another human being. Tears filled her eyes as she thought back on that night. It had started innocently enough. Just a few beers. Just a shot, and then another, and another. Soon the music flowed through her, making her swing her hips. A tall shadow fell across her as he stepped to her side. "Can I buy you a drink?" he asked. She smiled and blushed. She knew she should have said no, but a part of her just didn't want to. Drink after drink. He asked her to dance; she acted shy at first. He asked again. She blushed but relented. He was cute in his way; dark brown hair fell across his forehead as he danced with her. She blushed when he pulled her by her hips closer to him.

They danced this way for a while until she eventually pulled away to smoke a cigarette. He followed her outside and leaned against the wall. They flirted back and forth. She wasn't very good at it, but she never was. Eventually, he asked if she was with anyone in particular. "I'm married, but he is cheating on me." The lie left her lips before she could stop it. She was surprised at how easy it was. Had she changed that much?

He shook his head. "Sorry to hear that. I can't imagine anyone cheating on you." She grinned, embarrassed at his forwardness. Deep down, she loved it.

She was spinning out of control. In that moment, she wanted him as badly as he wanted her. A kiss in the back of her car and then another. She knew what she was doing was wrong, but she no longer cared. She needed him. An emotional tourniquet. Hoping it would stem the flow of utter despair bleeding from her hardening heart. His hands exploring her body until they eventually fell to her lap. She should have pulled away—she knew this—but she didn't want to. She wanted more.

Later, as she was pulling back on her jeans, she began crying softly. Who was she anymore? Tears fell onto her thighs as the guilt overwhelmed her. And then anger. What had Charlie done? Her hands shook with rage. How had he changed who she was? She swallowed hard and wiped her eyes. This was his fault. It had to be.

And then, as her memories faded and returned to the present, she was back in front of Charlie's. The windows were dark, reflecting her desperate soul. Again, the tears threatened to fall down her cheeks. She took a deep breath and composed herself. She stepped into the night to face yet another horrible, empty, soulless day of bitterness.

From the shadows, a pair of eyes watched as she climbed the stairs. The darkened form stood for a few moments and then sharply turned and disappeared into the night.

Chapter 12

A Mirror to the Soul

Dear Charlie,

Did you like the gift I left for you? I thought you might appreciate it. The girls were for you. You know that, right? What am I saying? Of course, you do. You're not like the rest of them; you get it. You're so smart. Sorry, I'm rambling. I am just so excited about finally speaking with you. I have followed your work for so long now I feel like I know you. I am a fan.

Oh my gosh. Where do I begin? I have tried to model myself after you as best I can. But it's hard. You're so reactive. I can't do that. I have to plan everything. If I don't, I am afraid I will get caught. I almost did, you know? They were so close in Illinois.

Anyways, I don't want to take up too much of your time. I just wanted to say hi. I would like to give you another gift. I am going to take care of something that I just know you will appreciate. And then we can meet. I just really think you will love it. It won't be long, I promise.

With the greatest respect,
An admirer

Chapter 13

The Tortoise and the Hare

Turtle sat at his desk, in the modest hotel room, running through the psychological profile that he built of Charlie based on the very little evidence, both in the letters and the cold cases that Chance's team had put together.

FEDERAL BUREAU OF INVESTIGATION
FREEDOM OF INFORMATION/PRIVACY ACTS
   SECTION
COVER SHEET

SUBJECT: CHARLIE

DECEMBER 5, 2018
UNSUB; AKA CHARLIE
SERIES OF HOMICIDES
DAYTON, OHIO
2018
NCAVC—HOMICIDE
(CRIMINAL INVESTIGATIVE
ANALYSIS)

The following criminal investigative analysis was prepared by Special Agent (SA) Dr. William

R. Tuttle, FBI National Center for the Analysis
of Violent Crime (NCAVC). At the request of
Captain Rashan Murphy from the Dayton Police
Force, in Dayton, Ohio, SA Tuttle was requested
to prepare an analysis of a series of unsolved murders occurring over several years.

SA Tuttle was provided background information relative to each case, as well as evidence
examined.

Victimology
In each homicide, the victim had a personal altercation with the attacker. This placed
the victims in a "high-risk" category. We define
"high risk" as someone who is very likely to be
the victim of a violent crime. By creating a hostile
environment, they made themselves a favorable
target to the assailant. There is no apparent pattern, race, gender, or class that seems to be being
targeted.

Medical Examination

1. No evidence of sexual assault.
2. With the exception of two attacks, the subject killed
    victims swiftly.
3. Subject was able to maintain control of victims
    during the initial "blitz-style" attack.
4. With the exception of two attacks, there was no evi-
    dence of physical torture prior to death.
5. Several attacks have shown evidence of possible man-
    ual strangulation.
6. With the exception of three attacks the blood was
    concentrated in small areas.

Crime and Crime Scene Analysis

Most victims were killed swiftly with no postmortem mutilation. There is no apparent pattern to the murders. With the exception of Officer Gershing's attack, no victim was left alive. Officer Gershing was left alive but heavily mutilated. After tracing the places where victims were attacked, there is no sign of the triangular pattern that is common amongst serial crimes such as this. The triangular formation is used as a secondary comfort zone for most subjects; however, Subject does not show an apparent need for a comfort zone. This may show signs of sociopathic tendencies. Some criminologists and behavioral scientists have written in the past that subjects will maintain their modus operandi, and that is what links so-called "signature crimes." This conclusion is incorrect. A subject will change his modus operandi as he gains additional experience. This is learned behavior. However, the personal desires and needs of the subject are expressed in the ritual aspect of a crime. The ritual is something that he must always do because it means he is acting out of the fantasy. This being said, I see no evidence of a ritual being used. This is highly unusual in these types of serial murders.

Communiques Received from "Charlie"

Another aspect of this case worth mentioning was the communiques allegedly received from Charlie. It is quite rare when a serial murderer of this type communicates with police, media, family, etc. When they do communicate, they generally provide specifics relative to the crime that only are known by the subject. In addition, they generally provide information relative to their motivation for committing such a heinous crime. It is my opinion that this series of homicides was not perpetrated by someone who set up a challenge against law enforcement. While the killer knew he would be receiving national as well as international publicity, this was not his primary motivation.

In summary, I would put emphasis on the communiques during this investigation. In addition, I would develop an investigative technique with the goal in mind to identify the author of the communiques.

Offender Traits and Characteristics

The offender does not look out of the ordinary. The clothing he wears at the time of the assault is his everyday dress.

He comes from a lower-middle-class family, with an emotionally abusive, domineering mother and an abusive father. As a result, he more than likely failed to receive consistent care and contact with stable adult role models. Consequently, he would have become detached socially and developed a diminished emotional response toward his fellow man. He became asocial, preferring to be alone. His anger became internalized, and in his younger years, he may have expressed his pent-up destructive emotions by setting fires and torturing small animals. By perpetrating these acts, he may have discovered increased areas of dominance, power, and control and learned how to continue violent destructive acts without detection or punishment.

As he grew older, his fantasies would have developed a strong component that included domination, cruelty, and mutilation of those who anger him. We would expect to find evidence of this violent destructive fantasy life through personal writings of his, as well as, possibly, drawings of people mutilated.

For employment, he would seek a position where he could work alone and vicariously experience his destructive fantasies. Such employment would include work as a butcher, mortician's helper, medical examiner's assist, or hospital attendant. He is employed Monday through Friday and on Friday night, Saturday, and Sunday is off from work. He more than likely carries a knife for defense purposes—just in case he was ever attacked, he would be ready.

This paranoid type of thinking is justified because of the poor self-image he has of himself. He would be expected to have some type of physical abnormality. However, although not severe, he perceives this as being psychologically crippling. We would look for someone below or above average height and/or weight. May have problems with speech, scarred complexion, physical illness, or injury.

We would not expect this type of offender to be married. If he was married in the past, it would have been to someone older than himself, and the marriage would have been for a short duration.

He would be perceived as being quiet, a loner, shy, slightly withdrawn, obedient, and neat, and orderly in appearance and when working.

The first homicide should be in close proximity to either his home or workplace.

Investigative and/or Prosecutive Techniques

Charlie would be best suited to be interviewed during the early morning hours. He
would feel more relaxed and secure to confess
to the homicides. He would feel more relaxed to
express himself by writing about his motivation
for killing the victims. He would not be visibly
shaken or upset if directly accused of the homicides. EOR...

Turtle smiled, pleased with himself, and shuffled the papers
together on the desk. It was cut and dry and full of conjecture, but
he felt like he may have hit the proverbial nail on the head with
the case study. Usually, when he was called in for this type of case,
his reports were fairly generic, but this killer was something special.
Charlie really broke the mold. Part of Turtle felt like an overexcited
child. He knew he shouldn't. These murders were particularly brutal,
but investigating a true sociopath was like following a rock star to a
psychologist.

Turtle threw the documents into his leather attaché and grabbed
his suit jacket. If he hurried, he could meet Tom downstairs at breakfast before they headed into the precinct that morning. He tapped
his inside jacket pocket with his hand to make sure he had his access
badge and buttoned the top button. He sipped his bitter hotel room
coffee and set it on the table before heading down to the lobby for
the continental breakfast that the hotel provided.

The lobby was surprisingly empty considering the time. But he
inwardly shrugged it off and went about loading his plate with the
unripened cantaloupe and overripened pineapple. He slipped two
bagel halves into the toaster and strummed the table with his fingers impatiently. As he waited a few people nodded politely as they
walked past him searching for the half-warm milk for their off-brand
cereals. Finally, the toaster springs threw the overcooked bagel halves
on to the top of the toaster. He rolled his eyes and headed to one of
the nearby tables.

After sitting at a table that someone had left that day's complimentary copy of the *Dayton Daily News*, he began the arduous task of trying to chew the almost two hard cantaloupe and flipped over the paper to the front page. There in large bold letters was the headline **"Charlie Knows if You Have Been Bad or Good**." Turtle gritted his teeth and read on. The entire story of Gershing was there, minus the contents of the letter, in every gruesome detail. The article almost sounded worshipful of the killer. Each sentence spun to sound as if he was doing the city a favor of getting rid of corrupt police officers. Of course, this was due in part to how the nation had been twisted into a frenzy over some recent shootings that had happened at a local Walmart and other public places. Even the end of the article was poignant, "So be good for goodness's sake." He furrowed his forehead in disgust and tossed the paper aside. If they were ever going to end this spree, the public would need to stop this undeserved hero worship. *Thank God the contents of the letter were not exposed*, he thought as he threw away his plate and cup and walked toward the front door.

As Turtle exited the front doors and turned to walk toward the parking garage, he had no way of knowing that peril was his shadow. A pair of piercing cold eyes watched him open his car door and drive away. The eyes fell away as the car drove out of sight and stared at the ground thoughtfully.

Chapter 14

Just Coffee, Thanks

Charlie stepped out of the cold and into the coffee shop. After finding an empty table close to the register, he removed his pea coat and hung it on the back of his chair. Tina buzzed about the register, staying busy cleaning counters and taking orders from the customers that sauntered in off the bitter-cold streets.

Charlie waited patiently for her to find time to take his order. A few minutes went by until he found a break in the crowd. "Hi," she smiled and brushed a strand of blond hair away from her face, tucking it behind her. He noticeably blushed and found himself searching for an adequate response, much like a lovestruck teenager. "What can I get you?" He struggled for a moment to remember what the manager had called his coffee, but finding himself at a loss, he offered "Black coffee please." She giggled and nodded. Charlie sighed, defeated, as she went about getting his order, knowing that he made himself sound like a simpleton. In today's trendy world, he often found himself stuck in the proverbial past. When finished, she handed him his scalding hot paper cup. Flipping it so he could read how badly she had misspelled his name, he was surprised to discover that not only had she spelled it correctly but had taken the extra time to draw stars and smiley faces bordering his name. Elated in this fact, he thanked her and returned to his lonely table.

Sipping the warm decoction, he stared reflectively out the window. The winter season had come quickly this year, pushing away the warm colors of fall. Their decaying remains gathered in the street gutters, gathering in small frost-covered piles on the curbs. Their complex reds, greens, and yellows marred by the impending winter tide.

His thoughts fell to Tammy. What had happened last night? Was there someone else? He frowned. Her inability to express herself only added to the stress and doubt creeping into his already weighted conscience. It was true that like most sociopaths, he had no remorse in his actions, but on some level, like a narcissist, he did worry about what the viewpoint of people close to him was. Above all else was Tammy's opinion. It cut deeply into his heart that she couldn't feel close to him as of late, and it was worrisome to think someone else may have stolen her heart. She had shown up extremely late from the bar last night. Was her need to avoid him so great that she was drinking more frequently to escape the imagined purgatory of just being in his presence?

Charlie shook his head to clear it of this negative thought, focusing on the people gathering around a television by the counter. They watched silent, in rapt amazement at the screen in front of them. Suddenly, a loud gasp escaped the lips of a heavily overweight woman toward the front of the crowd. Curiosity got the better of Charlie, and he stood to see what all of the fuss was about. On the screen, in vivid color, was a photo of the mangled, unrecognizable body of Officer Gershing. As the camera zoomed to his heavily bandaged face, the reporter went on to describe his amputated appendages. Low murmuring began between the people in the crowd. "Who could have done this?" "What sort of monster?" "Oh my gosh! How did he not die?"

Charlie frowned. He didn't like to think of himself as a monster; in fact, he thought himself to be more of a peacekeeper. The reporter interrupted his thoughts. "Officer Gershing is stable and is expected to pull through. Police officials have stated that this was an isolated incident and more than likely gang related. Several suspects have been brought in for questioning. WHIO Channel 7 news will keep you updated as we receive any details."

Gang related? Is that what they decided to tell the news? Charlie thought that they would credit him. At the very least, they would have listed why Gershing was attacked. He was the monster! Did they really not understand that? Or was this just another attempt at drawing him out into the open. Charlie pondered this as the crowd dispersed, leaving him standing awkwardly at the counter engrossed in his own world.

A voice drew him out of his melancholy fog. "Penny for your thoughts?" His eyes fell onto Tina's kind eyes.

"Oh, sorry. I didn't realize I was still standing there," he answered, embarrassed.

"It's okay, I was just worried about you. Pretty crazy, right?" she said, pointing up at the television.

He shrugged but agreed with her. "Yeah, good to hear he will pull through it okay." She nodded and started to turn away toward the register again. Desperate to keep her attention, he asked, "What do you think about it?" Inside, his stomach knotted up. What a stupid question. She would, of course, just nod and agree with him, but she surprised him by saying something he never expected.

"I don't know. I don't have anything against cops, but maybe he deserved it or something. Whoever did that to this guy wouldn't have gone to all of that trouble unless they wanted him to suffer. Sorry, that made me sound crazy, right?"

He was visibly taken aback. The shock must have shown on his face because she turned red and lowered her eyes from his, obviously regretting saying anything to him. He gathered himself and responded, as best he could, supportively. "I think you might be right! But why do it at all?"

She raised her face and pondered the question for a moment, until finally answering. "Well, maybe he was a bad cop or something? I don't know. I just know that after all of that, he was left alive on purpose. Personally, I would have finished the job. This seems like a vendetta thing, like they wanted him to live with it or to send someone else a message."

Charlie couldn't help himself; he smiled and nodded, enthusiastically agreeing with her. "I think you are on to something there!"

Reign it back in, he told himself. Nervous he would scare her off, Charlie composed himself and tried again. "Sorry, I just agree. I believe people often get themselves into situations that they could have avoided, if they were just a bit more self-aware."

She nodded agreeably and then continued, "Yeah, I think you're right. Either way, I don't believe it was gang stuff. We have a lot of drug problems here, but we don't really have that serious of gang activity. You know?"

He let a small smile escape the corners of his mouth and nodded. She impressed him with her intelligence and common sense. It wasn't very often that he found people who rivaled his own intelligence. They continued the conversation for a few minutes until Charlie noticed the time. He had a lot to do today. He apologized and asked for a to-go cup of coffee.

Charlie tugged his coat tightly around his athletic form, pushed the door open, and stepped into the bitter wind. There was much to accomplish today, and if he didn't hurry, he would miss his chance to find out who his secret admirer was. After a brief phone call, he smiled, satisfied with what he hoped would be a great outcome that evening. He smugly brought his coffee cup to his lips and took a sip. It was just the way he liked it, strong and black. As he lowered the cup, he noticed something written on the side. Just below Tina's name was a phone number with a heart.

Chapter 15

Dear John...

Charlie opened his front door and threw his keys on the table. "Tammy?" he called. "I'm home. How was your day?" No one answered. He searched the bedroom and returned to the kitchen confused. She was always home before him. He looked around for a note. On the fridge was a sealed envelope with his name written on the front. He grabbed it and went to the couch to read it. His hands began to tremble as he read these words.

Dear Charlie,

I told you once I was in love with you, and I was then. But now, although I love you still, I am not "in love" with you. I'm sorry, but you had to see this coming. I don't have the stomach to tell you to your face, so I will tell you why in this letter.

In short, we don't talk anymore. I feel strained trying to respond to your forced conversations. We just have nothing between us anymore. The thought of being with you intimately is hard to imagine anymore, and my kisses are hollow. I am sorry, but you brought it on yourself. I told you before you had dead eyes, and I don't want to look into them anymore. You say you can't change them and you're born that way, but you don't even try.

We had some good times, but I'm tired of trying with you. If I wait any longer, I will be too old to find someone else. I hope you understand. By the time you get this, I will be gone. I don't want to waste your time by saying we can be friends—it never works that way, and I don't feel like it, frankly.

Tammy

Charlie let the paper fall from his fingers onto the ground between his legs. A single tear fell onto the paper, staining the ink. He lay on his side, on the couch, and sobbed himself to sleep. It would be days before he would show his face to the world again. And they would regret it.

Chapter 16

And on the Seventh Day, He Rested

The sun snuck through the drawn blinds on Charlie's window and fell on his tear-stained face. His eyes strained against the brightness and he turned away. He had truly loved her. More than any man probably ever has about anyone else. Shakespeare couldn't have written a deeper affection. His body literally ached without her. It always had, and he had told her often. Perhaps too much, magnifying her lack of reciprocation. He would never understand this; it was incomprehensible. How can one man love someone so much and not be loved back?

He wasn't ready to face the world yet. It had been six days since he found the letter and had not even changed his clothes. Charlie had barely eaten anything. His stomach cramping, he finally drummed up enough energy to stumble to the fridge. Grabbing the jug of orange juice, he took a big swallow. Letting the sugar slowly reenergize him, he searched the counter for anything ready to eat. All he found was sliced bread. Grabbing the bread, he lowered himself to a sitting position against the cabinets and began eating it. He made it through one piece of bread and finished the bottle of orange juice. He pulled himself to his feet, and with his head hung, he headed to the bathroom to take a shower. One thing life had taught him was it wasn't what happened to you it was how you react to it.

The water fell across his muscular shoulders and dripped onto his feet. Charlie let the water temporarily wash away the soul-sucking sadness from the week. Yes, he would miss her. Every single day of his remaining life, he would miss her. But it would do no good to anyone to just sit there. She would never come back, he knew that, but he still couldn't keep hoping he was wrong.

As he sat there, letting the warmth of the water massage his stiff muscles, he tried to focus on the Chance situation. The hooker's killer had a fascination with him, of that there was no doubt. The letter he had received was almost a love letter: "The girls were for you." "Did you like it?" It was almost as if they were seeking his approval, which didn't fit the egotistical theme. The only difference between a sociopath and a psychopath was egotism; egotists don't need anyone's approval. Hero worship, he supposed, but how could he use that? The fact that the writer was trying to get at him through someone else was made obvious by the statement "I am going to take care of something that I just know you will appreciate. And then we can meet. I just really think you will love it. It won't be long, I promise." But whom? The only person Charlie could think of was Chance's girlfriend, Aryn. But he had a plan for that. He smiled assured in his scheme and turned off the water. He had a lot to do to set his trap in motion, but first, he had someone else to deal with.

Chapter 17

A Rose by Any Other Name

The doorbell rang its melodic tone across Chance's apartment, dragging the detective and his lover out of their dreamy slumber. Aryn groaned and threw a pillow over her head in sheer defiance of the visitor that was interrupting their peaceful rest. Chance stretched his arms above his body and threw his legs off the bed. His feet touched the cold wood floor, causing him to wince a bit. He looked over the edge of the mattress for his slippers. Finding them, he pulled himself out of the warm bed and made his way to the front door. Aryn watched him walk away and smiled. She pulled the comforting blanket up to her chin and soaked the last few moments of warmth she could get before being forced out of bed to face the day.

"How long has it been since I have been this content?" Aryn asked herself. Everything was going so well lately. It had been such a rough year before she moved here that this was almost unnerving. She had worked hard at getting this job here in Dayton, and thankfully, she was getting everything she had dreamed of. She smiled again and hugged her pillow.

Chance walked in, carrying a vase of flowers. Aryn giggled and jumped from the bed to wrap her arms around him. He gently pushed her away, confused.

"I appreciate it, but I didn't get these. A delivery guy just dropped them off for you." She stepped back and waited for Chance to place them on the nightstand before searching the flowers for a card. There between the delicate carnations was the ominous message,

I'm mostly chagrined of my inconsistency not greeting formally. Obviously Roning & You ought understand. Charlie.

She handed the note in her shaking hands to Chance, who read it, and then, in a fit of disgust, wadded it up and threw it to the ground. The silence that filled the room was deafening. Aryn sat on the edge of the bed, searching for strength to move in Chance's eyes, but none was to be found. In truth, Chance was at a loss. He felt lost, disgusted, and above all else, afraid. Fear is a horrible thing. It fills the corners of your soul and hides joy and love in its dark, cold shadow. It is both the protector from things unknown and the foreshadowing of incredible danger. One can sense impending danger in both an ending relationship or an impending attack, and they will feel the same. He could feel the clammy hand of death reaching for his shoulder. Up until now, Charlie had been, at most, a puzzle to be solved that threatened the citizens of Dayton, but now he was within Chance's private life. Charlie was watching him. And now it was personal.

The silence hung heavily in the air. Aryn was the first to recover and slowly rose to her feet, her legs rubbery and weak. Taking a deep breath, she addressed Chance. "How does he know about me, and exactly how does he know I'm here? Is he watching us?" Chance looked at her silently and snapping back into reality, he rushed to the front window and threw open the curtain, searching the street for anyone watching the house. No such luck was to be had as the street was empty; Charlie had obviously long departed. Chance rushed to the phone and called the flower company that delivered the seemingly deadly message. The delivery company was hesitant to give any information until it was explained that he was with the police department, after which they said that a man had come in and paid cash the day before. Chance frowned, knowing that there wouldn't be a way to track who it was electronically because a bank card was not used. As it had happened the day prior, all of the money had been deposited and by now had been lost in the shuffle at the bank. Chance sighed and asked the employees to come to the police station for further questioning.

Chance turned and watched Aryn, seemingly calmly, getting dressed and pulling on her shoes. Shaking his head to clear it from the anxiety, he rushed about the room, getting himself ready to head into the precinct. Grabbing his badge from the dresser, he hung it around his neck and turned to Aryn. "I have to head in and report this." She nodded in acknowledgment and leaned in for a long hug. He wrapped her in his muscular arms and kissed her forehead reassuringly. "It's going to be okay, we will get this guy. Can you come by the station later to make a statement?" he asked.

"Absolutely, I just have to take care of something first and then I'll be right over," she answered, allowing a slight smile to escape the corners of her mouth.

Chance left the room to grab his sidearm from the kitchen. What he didn't see, while waiting for his coffee to brew, was Aryn unwrapping the crumpled note and taking a photo of its contents with her phone. When he made it back into the room to escort her to her car, she made mention that he shouldn't forget to take it with him to the station. Nodding, he picked it up and placed it in a zip-lock bag to turn in as evidence. After walking her to the car, he kissed her and told her she was going to be okay. She nodded and said, "I'm not worried. It's going to take more than flowers to scare me."

She gave him one last kiss and closed her car door. As he watched her drive off into the distance, he was overwhelmed with the thought of losing her. They had grown so close over the last few weeks. He was, at that time, certain he was falling in love.

Chapter 18

He Followed Her to School One Day

Aryn drove in silence, thoughts of what to do next swirling about her mind like a whirlpool. Charlie was aware of her now. He was watching, and he had let her know. Paranoia would haunt her now, forcing her to subconsciously check her mirrors and avoid eye contact with people who pulled up beside her at stoplights. The speedometer crept ever higher as she drove through the city toward her office. The city laws on speed meant nothing to her as she rushed toward safety. She knew that she needed to write this story before the next day's newspaper was sent to the printer, and this screamed "headlines." A personal attack against a reporter meant that they were getting close to the truth. In truth, she had sought out Chance to get more information about Charlie but had grown to care for the detective. He was, in every way, the yin to her yang. The ever-righteous hero in this story called her life.

Morning shadows fell across the parking lot as she pulled into her spot. The leaves that had fallen from the trees lay dead and blowing slightly in the cool fall air. The city was still relatively silent as most of its citizens hadn't headed to work yet. She stepped out of the car and nervously lit a cigarette. A nasty habit, she had stopped two years ago, but as things go, the killings had caused pressure to print new headlines ahead of the wire. She stared down at her beige Alta, natural suede lace-up high heels, lost in thought. It was one thing to write about a killer from a distance, but to be personally linked with one was an entirely different story. How far away was he now? Was he watching? What did he know of her? These questions drowned her in anxiety. She could barely breathe, which was causing difficulty in enjoying her cigarette.

She shuddered, in part because of the brisk temperature and partly because of the overwhelming feeling of being watched. She stomped on the cherry of the cancer stick and turned quickly to head into the building. The welcoming warmth of the lobby felt oddly relaxing, and she took a deep breath and headed into the elevator to begin the short journey up to her office.

After sitting behind her desk, she waited for the computer to power on. Reaching into her purse, she grabbed her phone and read over the photo of the note from Charlie. There was something about it that stood out, but she couldn't pin down exactly what it was. Exasperated, she tossed the phone onto the desk and began searching through her notes on prior cases involving her stalker. After pinning down exactly what she wanted to write, she began tapping on the keyboard furiously. Each soft clack brought her closer to what she hoped would be an award-winning piece. Forty-five minutes later, she printed off the story and leaned back in her chair to review it. She read over the direct quote from Charlie's note and then smiled. She realized what was wrong.

Charlie stood outside, leaning on the wall of an Italian restaurant directly across the street from the *Dayton Daily News*. He couldn't see her from there but hoped that his rival would make an appearance. He pulled the drawstring closer around his face in an attempt to ward off the cold creeping in around his neck. It was getting colder; soon it would be winter and a dusting of snow would be a constant in this city. Never one to really be affected by seasonal affectedness disorder, he still found himself wishing he could be lying on a beach somewhere, enjoying the warmth of the sun as it slowly melted a tropical drink resting by his lounge chair. Maybe after all of this, he would make a trip toward warmer areas.

Charlie's attention was drawn toward a shadowy figure approaching him on his left. He watched as the man slowed to a stop and looked up at him. The man was clearly making a decision based on his facial expression, then with a look of resolution, he waved Charlie toward him. Charlie looked around for someone else that the man could have been signaling to, but alas, there was no one to be found. Charlie reluctantly pushed himself away from the wall and followed the man around a corner into an alley. As he rounded the bend, the man roughly grabbed Charlie and pressed a knife against his side. Charlie looked down at the dirty knife and tried to calm the anger and resentment rising up within him.

"Empty your pockets!" the man demanded nervously. Charlie slowly reached his hand into his pants pocket and withdrew his wallet. The man took it and pushed Charlie to the ground as he turned to walk away. If the man had just taken the money, Charlie could have controlled himself, but being knocked to the ground arose the animal within him. Charlie silently arose behind the man and removed his belt.

Aryn went to leave her office and headed toward Chance's precinct. As she pulled out of the parking lot, she noticed a small crowd gathered on the corner. As she pulled closer, she saw why.

Hanging from the parking meter, by a leather belt, was a man. Clearly dead, his face was cut from one temple to the opposite corner of his mouth. And on his chest was a single word written in blood: "Charlie."

Chapter 19

I've Seen Fire and I've Seen Rain

Tom Black and Turtle were huddled around the captain's desk when Chance knocked on the door. The captain looked up from the paperwork on his desk and waved him inside. Chance shook Tom and Turtle's hands and waited for an opportunity to update them on the morning delivery from Charlie. Before he could, though, Rashan stood and walked around to the door to close it. Avoiding Chance's eyes, he began speaking. "I dropped my paperwork today to retire."

Chance stood with the shock of what was just announced all over his face. "What do you mean, retire?" Chance asked, bewildered. It was true that the captain was getting up there in age, but he always seemed so energetic and youthful. Surely, he was joking.

"Yeah, I'm retiring," he responded while bowing his head and resting his hands on his hips. "It's been a long time coming, and with everything going on in the precinct, with Charlie and Gershing, I've had it. I'm done." He sighed sadly. Chance sat down and let it sink in. His friend, mentor, and savior was at an end with his career.

Rashan continued, "So anyways, it is going to be official in about a week, and they are looking for my replacement. You're the senior detective here, so I want to recommend you to take over as the captain." Chance looked up from his lap, speechless. "You would have to take the exam and sit in review for the position, but I think I have enough pull still to have you replace me, if you're interested."

Turtle rested his hand on Chance's shoulder and smiled understandingly. Chance had a big decision to make.

Finding his voice, he began speaking. "I'm honored, but I am a bit confused. Shouldn't they be bringing in a captain from another precinct?"

Rashan shook his head. "Not this time. Every precinct in the area is bogged down with Charlie's case. And to be honest, I can't imagine there are going to be many takers for the position in the middle of an active serial killer case. You have a lot to think about. I will let you get back to me about it by the end of the day."

Chance nodded and headed toward the door. It wasn't until he laid his hand on the door handle that he remembered why he had even come in that day.

Chance turned and began recounting everything that happened that morning while the agents and Rashan listened intently. He handed Turtle the bag with the note in it and waited patiently while the doctor put on sterile gloves before opening it. Slowly he unwrapped it, careful to not smudge any prints that may have been on it. After reading it silently, he handed it to Tom, who in turn read it and handed it to the captain. Almost as one, they voiced the same question: "Where is Aryn?"

It wasn't until half past twelve o'clock that Aryn arrived to fill out a sworn statement. Chance turned her over to a uniformed officer and waited at his desk until she returned. Normally, this was his day off, but with everything that had happened today, he felt it best to stay until all of the dust was settled. Not to mention that another report of Charlie had just been filed from the downtown precinct. He laid his head on his desk, lost in his thoughts, until he felt Aryn's hand on his back. He looked up and let eyes focus on her understanding face. "What's wrong, baby?" she asked. He frowned and began recounting everything that had happened in the captain's office. "What are you going to do?" Chance shrugged his shoulders and said he wasn't sure as of yet. She nodded and switched the topic to the murdered man outside of her office.

Chance stood up and angrily paced, back and forth, behind his desk. "What does he want from you?" he asked, exasperated.

HI, MY NAME'S CHARLIE

"Well, that's what I was going to tell you. I don't think that the flowers are about me—or even you!" she told him excitedly. "The beginning of each word spells out a message! I'm mostly chagrined of my inconsistency not greeting formally. Obviously Roning & You ought understand' translates to 'I'm coming for you!'" she explained. "If he wanted me or you to get that message, he would have just said that. It was sent to me because he knows I'm a reporter and was going to publish it. I think he wants to get the message to someone else!"

Chance took a deep breath and then pulled her close to him by the arm. "Are you telling me you published all of this?"

She pulled her arm away and stepped back. "Well, yeah! Of course I did. That's what I do! Besides, he sent it to me." Chance sat back down and picked up the phone to call the captain. After a brief conversation, he and Aryn were waved into the captain's office to join the agents.

Tom and Turtle listened intently to what Aryn had to say and then turned to the captain to discuss what should be done. "I say we pull the article before its run tomorrow," Tom said.

Turtle agreed but added, "However, perhaps we could use this to our advantage. What if we changed the message to say something else? It would infuriate Charlie and possibly drive him to leave another clue."

Rashan crossed his arms and silently contemplated the decision. After a few moments, he asked "What would the new message be?"

Turtle grabbed a sticky pad off of the desk and began scribbling different words down until he had come up with what he thought it should say. When the pad made it from person to person until it reached Aryn, it said, "I mostly want all improprieties to illustrate no guilt. Charlie."

Aryn nodded and circled the first letter of each word. "I'm waiting."

Chapter 20

The Captain's Last Day

Rashan had had a hell of a career, and it had left him both full of pride in his accomplishments and too tired to continue down the same path every day. Besides all of that, his wife had been nagging him to pull up roots and move down somewhere warmer than Ohio. Now that their children had all moved out, it was time to start a new journey, one where he and his wife could begin to enjoy each other again.

He kicked his shoes off and placed them neatly beside the front door of his house and leaned back into his easy chair. He had almost dozed off when his phone rang. "Hey, Captain, it's Chance. Is this a good time to talk?"

The captain listened, and a smile formed. "All right! Sounds great. I'll make the call right now! All right… Bye."

Rashan dialed another number and told the man on the other end that Detective Roning was his pick to take over as his replacement. Settling the receiver back into the cradle, he leaned back into his chair again and thought about his friend. He had watched over him like he was his own son; in fact, he loved him in very much the same way. He honestly couldn't think of anyone he would rather take over his precinct.

It wouldn't be for another half an hour that he would realize his wife hadn't come out and said hello. And yet another half hour before he would realize they would never say hello or "I love you" again.

As he arose to find out where his wife could be, he was struck from behind. Just as his eyes closed for the last time, a look of shocked recognition crossed his face—and then nothing.

Chapter 21

For Whom the Bell Tolls

Chance stood outside his friend's house, horrified at what he was going to find. The reports had gone out early in the morning. His son, fresh on his Thanksgiving break from college, arrived at his parents' house to do a load of laundry and found the bodies of both parents. The commissioner's voice still echoed with the news in Chance's ears.

"Detective?" a gruff voice interrupted his thoughts. Chance turned to face the commissioner himself. Shaking his hand, the detective followed the man into the front door. The living room looked like a Jackson Pollock painting. Blood had been sprayed about the room. And there under a white sheet was the captain, head beaten in with what clearly was the golf club beside his body. Chance swallowed hard and, after a moment, recovered his friend's face. He stood and asked where his wife was. The uniformed officers led them down the hall into the back bedroom. There, tied to the bed, was the lifeless body of Mrs. Murphy. She had been killed the same way that the prostitutes had, strangled with piano wire, and then had her eyes closed by the killer.

"Damn shame," the commissioner lamented. "He was the best of us, and his wife was a good woman."

Chance nodded, still not quite finding appropriate words to express his loss.

"I want this priority from here on out. Okay?"

Chance nodded and then spoke up. "Commissioner, I believe that this is related to the prostitute killer case we are working on right now as well, based on the similarities between the women's murders and Mrs. Murphy's body. I would like to work them both simultaneously until we can rule them unrelated."

The commissioner agreed and headed toward the door. As he passed the captain's body, he stopped, bent over, and pulled the badge off of Rashan's chest. "You should know, I received a call from the captain last night naming you as his successor. This is your position now, Captain. Make Rashan proud," he said as he placed it in Chance's hand. Chance took a deep breath and looked around the room, avoiding the commissioner's gaze, out of fear that he would lose his composure.

Chance pulled up in front of the precinct, parked, and then couldn't hold it in anymore. He cried. It wasn't the sort of tears that fall just because you're stressed but the type that fall when you've lost a father. Deep, guttural, almost painful sobbing. Rashan had meant so much to him, a true father figure, and to have him pulled from this earth like he had been was just too much. He took shallow breaths until he could contain himself and reached into his pocket to pull out the captain's badge. He ran his fingers over the blood-speckled metal and reflected on all the memories he had shared with his mentor. Finally, he pushed open the car door and headed inside.

Turtle and Tom were waiting for him inside of his new office. He wasn't quite ready to take Rashan's seat, so he sat across from them on the couch and explained everything that had just occurred, minus crying in his car. Tom and Turtle sat in silence until he had finished, barely an expression changing on their faces, sharing a quick glance. They both stood and made their way to the coffee pot. As they poured the hot black liquid into three different cups, Tom was the first to speak. "I'm truly sorry for the loss to the department. He was a good man."

Turtle nodded in agreement and handed Chance the third cup. Gratefully, he accepted it and took a sip. "Of course, you are now in charge of Charlie's investigation. How do you want to proceed?"

113

Chance spoke immediately. Something inside of him had cracked, and he felt like this was the time for action. Perhaps it was anger, or perhaps he was subconsciously using it as a distraction. Either way, he dove into his theory that Charlie wasn't the prostitute killer or, in fact, the captain's killer. It didn't fit his modus operandi. Turtle listened and nodded in agreement as it was explained to them.

So it was decided, from that point on, that Charlie would be investigated exclusively from the other open cases. Tom made a call to Washington, DC, and reported the current status of the case. After a brief conversation, he hung up and addressed the rest of the room. "Okay. So has the newspaper published our coup today?" Chance called out to the bullpen for someone to bring him the current day's paper. When it arrived, the front page had been printed word for word what they had decided. It was just a matter of time until Charlie would receive the same message.

Tom begged his apologies about having to leave to get some paperwork done, leaving Turtle and Chance alone. "I noticed you haven't sat behind your desk yet," Turtle said matter-of-factly. "Is there a reason?"

Chance sighed and acknowledged that he was right. "I just can't picture anyone else there but the captain."

Turtle nodded. "I understand, but you're the captain now, and nothing, not even waiting to sit behind his desk, is going to delay that. I am sorry for your loss, but it's time to take the reins." With that, Turtle stood up and headed toward the door. Chance sat in the silent room for a few moments and then headed around behind the desk. He slowly lowered himself into the chair and sighed. It was time to live up to what his friend knew he would. He laid his old badge on the desk and put the captain's badge on his chest. Tomorrow he would be wearing his dress uniform, but for today, this was good enough.

As he walked out of his office, mostly everyone stopped what they were doing and stared at him. And then, after what seemed like an eternity, they went back to work. And life continued.

Chapter 22

A Man Walks into a Coffee Shop

Charlie scanned the girls behind the counter of the coffee shop while he waited patiently in line to order. Tina was nowhere in sight, which was extremely disappointing, as he would have welcomed the distraction today of all days. After making his order, he headed toward his table in front of the window. Lying on the table was today's newspaper. On the front page were two stories. At the top was the shocking news of the captain of police's death, and then following that was Charlie's story. He read his story in depth, only to discover that the message he had left had been changed into a message for himself: "I'm waiting."

He smiled. "I know you are." He then began reading the captain's story and realized that this was just as much of a message as his story. How perfectly did this line up within the same day? The wife was killed in the same way as the hookers. His rival was circling. Nervous, reaching out, testing the waters.

"Hi, handsome!" a voice from beside him purred. He looked up into the greenest eyes he had ever seen. Tina's rosy cheeks were even brighter because of the cold outside. "Sorry, I ran out to grab more creamer. I was hoping you might come in today."

Charlie gave an awkward smile, saying, "I'm glad to see you too."

She smiled and took off her coat. "I don't start for about another fifteen minutes. Is it all right if I join you?" He felt his heart skip but readily agreed.

She laid her jacket on the back of the chair and sat down. She was so beautiful it was distracting. Blond hair, bright-green eyes, and a smile that could melt the snow. She had a body that wouldn't quit as well. Quite a bit younger than him, but it wasn't an awkward difference, at least between them. He stood for a moment to signal for more coffee and, in doing so, brushed his hand against her. A rush of what can only be called electricity shot between the two of them. It was like unfiltered animalistic passion for just a brief moment. Shocked, he looked back at her and realized she had felt it as well. As if those who were once strangers were reincarnated throughout the ages as lovers. The history of a thousand passionate nights was felt between them. He was so startled by it he pulled his hand quickly away and said his goodbyes.

She watched him as he left, just as confused and desperate to feel it again as he was. She took a deep breath, gathered herself back together, and dutifully headed back behind the counter to start working again. And as she served the customers their lattes and coffees, her mind never left that moment.

Charlie buried his hands deep in his jacket pockets and hurried away. He felt both guilty and elated at the same time; it was an odd feeling. Tammy had just left him; it was too soon. Even though she was done with him, he still felt like he was cheating on her in some way. He was sad but also relieved to see that he could be reawakened again in this way. His heart had been cold, and he felt as if he was getting through each day almost robotically. However, when he was with Tina, he could see a future he never thought was possible again.

But before he could pursue Tina, he needed questions answered by Tammy. Speaking of which, where was she? Even in the worst break-ups, there is usually some contact. Tammy hadn't even asked to come by and grab the stuff she had left at his house. It was odd. Most of friends were reluctant to speak about her, if they even in fact knew where she was. Perhaps it was time to track her down and try and move past this.

As he walked, he became aware that his leg was wet. He looked down; there on his pants was a bloody patch. The wound that he had received yesterday from his attacker, in the struggle, had bled through the bandage. In an attempt to cover the blood spot and his guilt, he took off his jacket and wrapped it around his waist, with the back of the jacket facing his front. He limped to his car and got in before too many people noticed. The incident with his pants helped to remind him that he needed to get rid of the knife that he had stashed in his car. He reached underneath his seat and grabbed the hilt. He shoved it into the inside pocket of his jacket to get rid of later.

As he drove off to his house to change both his bandage and his pants before heading into work, he contemplated how to best find out where Tammy was. She had yet to answer any of his messages and, from all appearances, hadn't been back to her apartment. Of course, he could always wait outside her apartment or work, but that was creepy, even for him. His mind drifted back to Tina as he rolled down the road.

Chapter 23

Gershing's Revival

As men are apt to be babies when we are hurt or sick, Gershing was no exception. Not that he didn't have a reason to be. No tongue, and severe trauma to both ears. The doctors had managed to save the hearing in one ear, but it would be a waiting game to see if the other ear would recover. His hands had multiple surgeries, and although the hands were horribly shattered, they managed to set them. How well he would be able to use them would also be up to Father Time.

He spent most of the day listening to the television out of the somewhat repaired ear. Waiting for the next nurse to help him go to the bathroom and feed him. He was in constant pain, but the nurses kept him drugged regularly, so it wasn't intolerable. A familiar voice beside him drew his attention. Turtle had made the trip out to see him, with Tom in tow. "Officer Gershing? Can you hear me?"

Gershing nodded painfully.

"This is Dr. Turtle, one of the agents that you were working with. I need you to answer a few questions. Nod if that's okay."

Another nod.

"Okay, great. The night that you were attacked, did you get a good look at your assailant?"

Nod.

"Okay. Was he Caucasian?"

Nod.

"Did he have brunette hair?"

Gershing shook his head.

"Was he a blonde?"

Nod. Tom furiously scribbled notes as Turtle continued the questioning. It went on this way until Gershing's nurse came in to change the dressings.

As they were leaving Tom looked back to witness what used to be a large bully of a man being changed like an infant. It would have been ironic, if it weren't so sad to witness. "Damn." Turtle just shook his head in agreement and continued down the stairs.

It wasn't until they made it back to Captain Roning's office that they discussed their notes. Chance called to have a sketch artist sit in to try and draw up a rough sketch of who Charlie was. Tom read back the notes word for word, but at the end, the sketch was very nondescript. According to Gershing, Charlie had absolutely no distinguishable traits other than race and color of hair and eyes. At least of the questions that Turtle had time to ask. The age was interesting, though. Because although Gershing had indicated that he was in his late twenties, it didn't fit the psychological profile at all. Charlie should be in his mid to late thirties.

Chance made a photocopy of the sketch and hung it up on his wall as a motivator. It wasn't much to go on, but it was more than they had yesterday. Chance loosened his tie. He wasn't used to wearing his dress uniform all the time, and the starched collars still irritated his neck. He spent most of his days fielding calls between the commissioner and avoiding the press. He was starting to realize why his old friend wanted to retire. This thought saddened him. And he turned away from Charlie's sketch to speak with the agents.

Turtle seemed enthusiastic about the results. "I'm pretty sure we can do better with further questioning, but this was a great start." Tom nodded, but in truth, he wasn't as assured as his partner. "I guess we can head back over there in the morning. Captain, have you spoken with Aryn lately?"

"Yeah, I saw her this morning. Why?" Chance asked.

"Has she received anything else or gotten any calls?" asked Tom.

"Not as of yet," Chance answered.

Tom shook his head and started packing up his briefcase. "I think I might head over there and ask her a few follow-up questions." At first, Chance was annoyed that the Agent felt that he had to follow up after him, but it was their show essentially, and it was possible that he and his men had missed. So reluctantly he agreed and said good-bye to the two gentlemen.

Chance had other things he had to focus on. He put up copies of all of the letters he had received from Charlie up beside the new sketch. He stared at them, trying to see if there was some sort of code. Charlie had shown that he was capable of that in the past, so it was possible that it was in the other letters. But try as he might, he could find nothing. However, the recent discussion about Gershing did make him ponder a bit about the first letter. Charlie had asked for him by name to be involved in the investigation. He had singled him out. Was it possible he already knew of Gershing's outright disturbing past? Maybe it was his way of finding a way to get him alone long enough to punish him. That would be extremely calculating. And as he thought of that, it dawned on him that Charlie could have just cut off Gershing's hands. Why just break them? It would be extremely risky that he would be able to use them again. Chance leaned back in his chair and pondered this until his phone rang and he was drawn back into his normal duties.

A storm was brewing as the agents drove toward the *Dayton Daily News* building. Heroin addicts and meth heads scattered under overhangs in hopes of avoiding getting too wet from the approaching storm. Tom shook his head. He never understood how people could fall so far down in life. And it wasn't from limited experience either. His sister was also a heroin addict. He had let her live with him and his now ex-wife while she was trying to "get better." This ended up putting unneeded stress on their relationship and eventually ended the marriage. His sister would wait until he was asleep and invite other men over to watch her strip for money. It was the final straw. Not that he didn't love her; it was just too hard to look at her anymore. She had caused a relationship to end that he valued more than any other. Turtle had a different perspective. His background in psychology put a different viewpoint in his path. He realized that pain medication, which is readily prescribed by doctors, leads to drug dependency, which eventually leads to different and harder drug use.

Most of their rides were silent like this. Both men were comfortable enough with each other that they could simply be in one another's company. They had worked together for two years now and, in general, knew what one another were thinking at any given time. Much like a married couple. Tom's former partner, Mitch Chandler, was one of a kind. He was always the first through a door when danger was imminent, but that was what had ended his life far too soon. It took Tom quite a while to accept new partners after that. Turtle was fresh out of his doctoral program at Wright State University when he attended Quantico and was assigned directly to Tom. Almost immediately, the two hit it off. Where Mitch was headstrong and often reckless, Turtle was methodical and careful.

It wasn't long until they were standing in the lobby waiting for Aryn to join them. She came from the elevator, a true beauty to behold. Pink pleated skirt with a loose-fitting white blouse accented her hazel eyes. She shook both Turtle and Tom's hands and led them into a nearby conference room.

The pleasantries at an end, Tom led the questioning while Turtle took notes. "Has there been any further contact with Charlie?" he asked.

She said no.

"Have you received any more gifts or notes of any kind?"

"No."

"How long have you been in the area?"

"About ten months."

"Where did you come from before that?"

"Chicago."

Tom could feel Turtle questioning something in his mind, but he continued. "How long have you known Captain Roning?"

She hesitated for a moment and then explained "I met Chance in high school, but we didn't hang out much then."

Tom turned to Turtle because he could sense that he wanted to ask a question. "Aryn. Can I call you Aryn?"

She nodded yes, so he continued.

121

"Why did you move to Dayton?"

"Originally, I was covering the society pages, and I was looking for a change, not much chance for advancement in that type of writing," she explained.

"Was there much of a pay difference between the two? I'm just curious," he asked.

Tom hid his confused face behind a cup of coffee but waited for her answer.

"Actually, I took a decrease switching to Dayton to write, but the cost of living is lower," she answered, smiling. Turtle nodded and let the subject drop. Tom continued to question her, but it was mostly just fact-checking over the original report. When he was finished, she bid them farewell and quickly walked away to get back to work.

For a full ten minutes, they sat in silence until Tom broke the silence "Why were you asking her about Chicago?"

Turtle answered, "Aren't Detective Merring and Officer Gershing both from Chicago as well?"

"Yeah, they are, if I'm remembering correctly," Tom agreed.

"Well, it's interesting that she moved around the same time that Charlie was being investigated, not to mention how many of the investigators on the same case are also from Chicago," Turtle mused.

Tom didn't reply but saw where Turtle was going with it. It was, at the very least, a coincidence and it warranted looking into. Maybe a call to her last paper was in order.

The station was wrapping up for the evening, and the night shift was starting to shuffle in when they arrived. Chance had already left, and seeing there was no more they could do that day, they decided it was time to call it, and go get dinner. But somewhere, in the back of their heads, they continued to think about Aryn's interview.

Chapter 24

The Merry Men

Pullman, Merrings, and Truman had been busy themselves. While Chance and the two agents had been doing the investigation from the office, they were out on the streets trying to get what information they could get from their sources.

Just now, they were headed out to one of Pullman's plug sources. He had received a call that the plug had some new information on Charlie. As people who are involved in the sale of drugs are often rue to give information to police, Pullman reasoned it must be fairly valuable information, so he had grabbed the rest of the team and headed toward Beavercreek, a superb of Dayton.

Radio traffic was high as they drove. It was the end of the month, so the traffic cops were trying to up their traffic citation numbers before they were turned in. The radio hissed in between each call in, and Merrings turned it down to avoid the inevitable headache. "What's this guy's deal?" he asked Pullman.

"He deals coke and weed mainly. When I busted him, he was dealing meth, had his scales and $1,000 cash too," Pullman explained. "He cut a deal with the DA to turn his suppliers in, and we keep that quiet on the streets as long as he keeps giving us info. If it's good enough, we throw him a little cash."

Truman, who had been sitting quietly, spoke up. "Hey, how do you guys feel about Chance taking over for the captain?" Truman shrugged.

"I like the guy, and he will probably do a good job. Would have liked to have been in the running too, but I get it. Why?"

"I don't know. I think I still haven't completely accepted that the captain is dead," Truman said, followed by a loud sigh.

"Why didn't you apply?" Merrings asked Truman.

"Not my bag of tea," Truman said and stared back out the window. In fact, Truman did throw his hat into the ring, but sometimes things just don't work out the way we hope. He had been on the force the longest, but he wasn't next in line, Chance was, and Truman tried to keep that in mind. He continued to think about it until they pulled up in front of Stan's Donuts, a local fixture in the community.

They walked in, and sitting in the corner was Pullman's plug. Pullman squeezed into the bench beside him while the other two sat opposite. "How you been, Will?"

The man beside him winced; he preferred to use his street name. "It's Chunk."

Pullman rolled his eyes and shifted back into his bench. "Fine. Chunk. What do you have for us?" Chunk was a slender but tall man covered head to foot in different tattoos. Huge white plugs hung in his earlobes. Holes still showed where he used to wear facial piercings, but age had taught him wisdom in not wearing them. On his bald scalp was a hat that had a lawn care company's name on it. After a one-year stint in the state penitentiary, he started a business to try and go straight. Unfortunately, like most ex-cons, it's extremely difficult to keep on the straight and narrow because people don't want to give them a chance. In order to supplement his income from landscaping, he still sold minor drugs to friends and family.

"So I got my dude, right? He came by and he, um…was in an altered state, got to telling me that he saw that dude who got his face cut robbing a white dude. Saw what he was wearing and everything."

Truman signaled for the waitress and then leaned in, lowering his voice to almost a whisper. "All right, what you got?"

"So this dude tells me that the guy has yellow hair and is wearing jeans and a red jacket. When he walks around the corner, he sees him on the ground. The dude gets up, and my boy thinks he's going to run away, but he doesn't. He starts taking off his belt and strangles the other dude from behind. Then when the other dude is dead, he doesn't stop—he just keeps pulling on the belt. Then he pulls out a knife and cuts dude's face after he was dead!"

Chunk stopped to let it sink in while the waitress poured the men coffee and took their donut orders. After she was out of earshot, he continued. "So anyways, this guy hid behind a dumpster until after the white dude started leaving, but he saw him put the other dude's knife in his coat. And when he started dragging the dead guy to the street, you could see his leg was bloody. He must have gotten stabbed while he was strangling the guy."

The detectives were stunned. A witness to one of Charlie's murders, finally! "So where can I find this guy?" Pullman asked.

"Man, I can tell you that! Then everyone will know that I'm talking to you guys! Come on, dude," Chunk protested.

Pullman and the other detectives looked at each other. It was true if they tracked down the witness, it would burn their source. Now they had a difficult decision: it was either lose future arrests or get one step closer to their captain's murderer. Truman was the first to speak. "Look, we don't give a damn what happens to you frankly. We have one cop in the hospital and our captain and his wife are dead now. Now give us the name, and we will try and pick him up on something else and get the info from him that way. But if I have to, I'll burn you myself!" he finished sharply.

Chunk shook his head, annoyed. "Fine, man, whatever. His name is Matt, Matt Nachbauer. He's usually down under the third street bridge smoking."

Truman nodded then stood, throwing a fifty-dollar bill on the table. "Pay for the donuts, and then keep the change." Then he grabbed his last donut and led the other detectives out the door. Chunk cursed under his breath and looked out the window, wondering how he was still in this life.

Twenty minutes later, the detectives pulled under the bridge. Merrings stepped out and called out. "Matt?" No one answered, but several people walked away from a group, leaving only one man standing alone.

Merrings walked over to him and asked again, "Matt Nachbauer?"

"Yeah," was the response.

"Why do I smell weed, Matt?" asked the detective as he turned him around and had Matt put his hands on his head. A quick pat down revealed a one-hitter and a small bag of weed. "Uh-oh, Matt! What's this?" Merrings asked sarcastically.

"Shit, man, that's not mine. I'm wearing my brother's pants!" the man lied.

"That's fine, brother. Why don't we take a ride downtown and we will get your brother to bring your pants?" Merrings read him his rights and then placed him in the back seat with Truman. Truman immediately complained about the man's body odor. Merrings and Pullman chuckled and drove away, Truman complaining the rest of the way.

Chapter 25

The Noose Is Getting Tighter!

It wasn't long before the detectives had squeezed out a witness statement from Matt in return for having the possession charges dropped. They even managed to make him think he gave up the information on his own accord, instead of selling out Chunk.

Two hours later, the three detectives were in Chance's office giving him the rundown of what had gone down. Chance listened intently. This was the lead they were looking for. After they were finished, he asked them to make the calls to all the local clinics and hospitals to see if they had received a wound like Charlie's on that day. Pullman and Merrings left Truman behind and went out to start making the calls. After the door closed, Truman stood up and said, "Hey, Captain, I just wanted to say I'm proud of you, and I'm glad to see you move up."

Chance smiled and took his hand warmly. "Thank you, I really appreciate it. It's been hard, I'm not going to lie. Sometimes I still feel like I am invading his space."

Truman nodded understandably. "You'll be all right, just keep doing what you're doing, kid." He smiled and walked out. Chance watched his mentor and thought about how much things had changed recently, and at the same time, things seemed the exact same at moments.

The phone rang. "Dete…Captain Roning," he awkwardly corrected himself.

"Hi, baby!" Aryn greeted him.

"Oh, hi! How's work going?" She told him everything was great and then asked if he was free for dinner. His plans set for the evening, he hung up the receiver, then after some thought, he picked back up his phone to call the agents and let them know they had a better description of Charlie.

The next day, Charlie was sitting at his table when he picked up the newspaper. There on the front page was a sketch of his face, along with a fairly detailed description of him! Frustrated, he folded the paper back up and tossed it on the table. Staring out the window, he could feel his anxiety rising. He always knew it was just a matter of time before somebody would see him. How he had been so lucky in the past he would never know. Sure, he was always very careful, but you can only get away with these things so long. Sighing, he picked back up the paper and stared at the rough sketch again. It was similar, but how similar? Nobody was paying any particular attention to him.

The line had dwindled down to just a few patrons at the coffee counter, so he grabbed his empty cup and headed to the counter to get a refill and speak with Tina. She had her hair down today, cascading across her delicate shoulders. Her wide, beautiful green eyes sparkled at the ends of her perfect smile as she looked up from her register at him. She reached out and let her hands rest on his, just a brief moment, as she took his cup. "Another coffee?"

He smiled, something he wasn't accustomed to. He had been smiling a lot lately ever since meeting her. He was so overwhelmed with the thought he couldn't help but ask, "Would you want to grab some dinner with me tonight or something?"

Suddenly, he realized how forward that was and instantly regretted it. She looked around her shocked but said nothing. Hanging his head, he mumbled an apology and walked quickly away to his table. "What was I thinking?" he mused as he rolled his eyes. "She never told me she was interested or anything."

He stared out into the cold streets, trying to distract himself from the epic failure. But then, before he even recognized what was happening, Tina had sat down in the chair beside him. In her hands, she held the coffee he had left behind in his embarrassed retreat. She blushed as she spoke, "I, um, was just surprised earlier. I think that would be cool!"

It was Charlie's turn to blush.

"Where were you thinking we would go?" she asked.

Now where to eat was never in question for Charlie. He could Mexican food any day of the week. "How about at Don Patron's in Beavercreek?" he asked.

"Oh, I love Mexican food! I get off at around five today, want to meet at seven?" He shyly agreed, and after a little more pleasantry, she stood to leave, excited for the night's plans.

Chance smiled and drank the last of his coffee before leaving the shop. He smiled, happy with himself, as he walked toward his car to leave. Behind him, from the window, Tina watched him walk away. A faint sign of a limp impeded his usually smooth gate. Lost in her thoughts, she began cleaning the table. As she finished, she flipped over the newspaper to see the front page. Thoughtfully, she looked back again as Charlie drove past. Then she folded the paper again and placed it under her arm.

On the opposite side of town, Aryn was frantically typing away at her computer in her office. Ever since the message from Charlie had arrived, tucked neatly among carnations, she had started working in more earnest. She had become more passionate in her endeavor to uncover just who he was. A recent tip had come through, that a man who fit the most recent description frequented a coffee shop downtown. As the call had come directly to her as opposed to the police, she wanted to be the first to verify this before the police were able to censor her. But before she could head over, she needed to send a quick update to her editor. Her cell phone buzzed silently on her desk. Looking up to see who it was, she purposely ignored it.

Chance sighed and hung up his cell phone and replaced it in his pocket. He hadn't been able to get hold of Aryn since after their dinner the night before. Their date seemed to go well, but when usually she accompanied him back to his apartment, this time would be different. After he paid the bill, she politely kissed him and said goodbye, promising to call him later. This would not happen. Was it something he had said? Or, perhaps, something he didn't say? Chance was never the best at knowing how to handle the opposite sex, especially conversationally. However, with Aryn, it always seemed natural. Of course, he was sure she had a lot on her mind with the most recent demand for updates on the Charlie investigation. Whatever the problem might have been, it bothered him greatly now.

"Captain?" came Merrings's voice from the doorway.

"Yeah, what's up?" Chance asked, gesturing to the chair.

After they both had seated, Merrings began speaking. "I was just called by my contact at the *Dayton Daily*. Apparently they received a tip that someone has seen Charlie at one of the coffee shops down on Main street. You want us to go ahead and look into it?"

Chance said nothing at first and just stared up at the ceiling, confused. Why hadn't Aryn said anything about a tip? It was possible, although not probable that she didn't know about it yet. But she was the lead reporter on this. Maybe, just maybe, that's why she was avoiding him. "Yeah. Actually, let's go down together. Just me and you," Chance decided.

Merrings nodded and went to go grab his jacket. Chance switched out his dress uniform to plain clothes and went out to join Merrings in the car. The last thing he wanted to do was draw attention to the coffee shop, on the off chance this was a valid lead.

Forty minutes later they were standing in front of the manager of the coffee shop. "I just got done talking to the newspaper lady!" she griped. Chance turned his head slightly to hide an eye roll. Of course she had. It looks like Aryn was holding out on him again.

"Sorry about that. If you could tell us the same thing, you told her we would appreciate it," Merrings said, trying to soothe her.

"Well, this guy comes in every day and gets his coffee and sits over there looking out the window. He looks just like the newspaper drawing of that guy Charlie everyone's looking for," she informed them.

"Okay. What time does he come in?" Merrings asked.

"Around eight."

Nodding, he added it to his notebook and then asked, "Is there anything you can add to the description that isn't in the newspaper?"

She shook her head but then stopped and angled her head toward a girl behind the counter. "He talks to Tina a lot."

Chance took that cue to break away from the conversation and speak with the girl the manager had indicated. "Hi. Tina, is it?" Chance asked the blonde.

"Um…yeah?" she nervously answered. "My name is Captain Roning, I'm with the Dayton PD." He showed his badge as he introduced himself. "I understand that there's a guy who comes in each morning who looks like this?"

He pointed to the sketch in the newspaper. She looked at the sketch but shook her head. "I mean he looks kind of like that but not too much."

Chance noticed that she seemed in a hurry to move past the topic, but he pushed on. "Well, we still need to follow up on every lead. Did he come in today?"

She reluctantly nodded.

"Okay, was there anything odd about him? Maybe a scar or a recent injury?"

Hesitantly, she started to nod, thinking of Charlie's slight limp, but then changed her mind and answered, "Not that I saw."

Chance took note of her odd behavior. "Okay, no problem. Thank you for taking time to speak with me," he said as he turned to walk away, then he stopped short and turned back. "One last question, ma'am. Would you feel comfortable in a room alone with the man we are talking about?"

She thought about that for a moment, and then with certainty, she answered, "Absolutely."

He nodded and then said goodbye and joined Merrings as he waited by the door to leave. Tina could overhear him say, "Have an unmarked stake this shop out tomorrow. I have a feeling this is our guy."

Chapter 26

A Date with Destiny

Charlie looked at the menu. He wasn't sure why. A creature of habit, he only ordered the same thing every time, steak fajitas. He signaled the waiter to bring him a pina colada and looked at his watch, Tina was fifteen minutes late. Annoying. It wasn't that he minded waiting, but it seemed like the politeness of calling people when one was going to be late had gone out the window about ten years past. Online dating has taken out personal responsibility in relationships. He sighed and looked toward the door.

Outside, Aryn sat in her car, debating whether or not to join Charlie. Something about him both excited and worried her. The chances of him being a serial killer were very low, but the sketch in the newspaper was a dead ringer for him. She nervously drummed the steering wheel before taking a deep breath and opening the car door to head into the restaurant.

He smiled as she nervously sat down across from him. "Hi! I was beginning to wonder if you decided not to come," he said.

"Yeah, I'm really sorry. It ended up taking longer than I thought," she lied.

"That's fine. How was work?" he asked, switching topics. She looked at him. Surely this unassuming young man couldn't be the man everyone was hunting for. She let her guard down a bit and leaned in a bit closer to tell him about her day, purposely leaving out the bit about the police. He forgot all about her lateness as he listened intently. Their conversation grew past just pleasantries as they waited on their food and drinks to arrive. And so it was with most dates; as their conversation deepened, their bond grew ever closer. The drinks sat heavy with them, and it lessened the worry that he was dangerous. They spoke of each other's current lives and their dreams and hopes for the future. They spoke about what their favorite colors were and their ex-relationships. It was both wonderful and full of wonderful possibilities at the same time.

Four drinks in, she laid her hands on top of his, and before she knew it, she was rubbing his fingers with hers. He was charming but shy; it drove her wild. He was suddenly aware of just how much he had missed physical touch. Her soft touch sent vibrations throughout his entire body. She giggled and then said, "I didn't say anything about this earlier but my manager called the newspaper today and said that you matched a description of that serial killer everybody's been reading about." Suddenly, Charlie could feel a lump in his throat. It was just a matter of time now. He would be caught and all his work to find the other killer would be for naught.

"Oh yeah?" he asked, masking his anxiety with a smile. "Yeah, it's silly, but a reporter came in and then some police and asked us about you. I told them I didn't believe it was you, but they said they were going to watch the place." He laughed and brushed it off, but it left him considering just what to do. If he went back there then he would be caught, but if he didn't return, Tina would know he was that Charlie. He began to feel like his collar was tightening. He realized that in every way Tina was going to find out no matter what he decided. The thought of her finding out broke his heart. He had to be the one to tell her.

They finished, and he paid the bill. As they were leaving, he asked, "Can I walk you to your car?" She smiled and took his hand, leading the way into the parking lot toward her car. She leaned against the door and waited for the inevitable kiss good night.

He leaned toward her and summoned up the strength, he began, "Tina, I have something I have to tell you."

Confused as to why he hadn't just kissed her, she waited for the rest. "Earlier, you were talking about the police coming to talk to you, and you said that you didn't think it was me. It is me," he admitted gloomily.

Her heart dropped into her stomach, and she let his hand drop. She felt fear creep up the back of her neck, and she froze in place. He began again, "I don't know how to say this, but I wanted you to hear it from me instead of finding out tomorrow when I didn't come in. I'm not as bad as you think I am. I only kill people who really deserve it, like molesters and rapists."

Her eyes wider than they had ever been, she was seized with the overwhelming desire to flee, but her legs wouldn't obey her brain that screamed, "Run!"

Chance could see how much she was afraid and hated it. He never wanted anyone to find out, least of all this woman. Not knowing what else to say, he said, "I would never hurt you. And I promise I have never hurt an innocent person." Questions swirled in her mind. Chance seeing her confusion encouraged her to ask questions.

She scanned the parking lot for someone, but seeing no one, she bid her time and nervously asked, "What about the prostitutes?"

She held her breath, waiting for his answer. "No, I swear. I have never killed a woman."

"What about the captain's wife?" she asked accusatorily, not meaning to.

"I didn't touch either one of them," he responded. Something about his eyes made her believe him. "There's someone else out there killing these people and blaming it on me. I think they are trying to get my attention. That's why I can't go in tomorrow. If I get caught then, whoever it is, will get away with all of this. I'm the only one who can end this," Chance explained and waited for her response. She stared at him silently. She didn't know what to say.

"I know that you need to process this. If you never want to see me again, I understand," he said, choking back the lump forming in his throat. "I'll let you go. I just didn't want you to find out from anyone else." She shook her head, and he stepped back to let her get in the car. She closed the door and fumbled with the keys, purposely avoiding his gaze. He watched as she pulled away sadly.

When she felt like she was safely away, she pulled out her phone and started to call the police. But before she dialed the last number, she stopped. Something in his eyes let her know that she had nothing to fear from him. Her brain screamed to her that she needed to turn him in before he could kill again, but her heart stopped her. She wasn't sure why; she just knew she wasn't going to. A single tear fell from her eye onto her blouse. For now, his secret was safe with her.

Chapter 27

The Elision

Like music, in life there is sometimes an elision. An elision is a section of music that different sections overlap each other. It builds tension and drama. So was the day that followed.

A letter laid upon Charlie's car window, tucked beneath his wiper blade.

My dearest Charlie,

As I write this, I am reminded of the message you left me. I'm coming for you. The moment I realized what you meant my heart raced. I have been looking forward to that so much, but unfortunately, while it's not yet our time, it soon will be. I know you like to have control because I do as well, but this isn't something you have control of. This time, I have everything planned, and soon, I'll decide just when to meet you. By the way, in case you haven't figured it out (I'm sure you have, you're so smart!), I didn't write you the message in the newspaper. It was the police. I worried that it would draw you out and lead them to catch you, but the more I thought about it, the more I knew you would never go that easy. Of course, you knew that wasn't me!

Oh! I am so excited! Just a bit more and we will be together. I suppose you have been wondering where Tammy is. And I am truly excited about this, but Tammy is with me. She's fine for now—a bit too sassy for my taste, but I'll give her as a gift to you when we finally meet. You could never have hurt her yourself, so I will do it for you. You are so welcome. Deep down you want me to. Anyways, I have a few more things to take care of.

See you soon,
Your truest friend

Disgusted, Charlie folded the letter and roughly shoved it into his pocket. So that was where Tammy had disappeared to. As much as she had hurt him, he had no desire to see her hurt. If she was in the hands of this psycho, then it was just a matter of time before she was dead. As cold as it was, he started to sweat. The thought of what this person was going to do to her or what had already been done to her was too much to bear. The only solace he had now was that the letter said she was alive. This meant that there was a chance he could get to her first. What to do now?

It was unsettling for him to change his routine of getting coffee before heading to work. He knew it was necessary, but it still bothered him that his sanctuary had been desecrated by the police. His phone vibrated. There on his Snapchat was a message from Tina. It read, "I missed you today. But I thought a lot about what you said, and I decided that I wouldn't tell anyone. I know why you didn't come in. I don't know what I'm thinking, but I can't stop thinking about you and I need to see you again."

Trembling, he typed back, "I have been so worried about what you were thinking. I wouldn't have blamed you for telling anyone. I had a wonderful time last night, and I can honestly say I have never felt this way about anyone." As he sent it, he could see that she was reading it, but alas, there was no response. He closed the screen on his phone and tossed it into the empty cup holder, but then as an afterthought, he checked the time on his radio before turning his car back toward downtown. Perhaps he would get some coffee after all.

Outside of the coffee shop, in her car, Aryn watched the crowd from a safe distance. It was just a matter of time, and Charlie would arrive to sit at the front table. Unbeknownst to her, the police were watching the shop as well. In particular, they were watching Tina. They could see her place her phone back in her pocket and, with her mind clearly involved in something else, continue to get the various fancy coffees for the other customers. It wasn't long before a man limped toward the front of the café and sat down at the table. As he sat down, he twisted the cup toward the window so that Aryn and the police could see the name *Charlie*. The scarf about his neck obscured his face, but his height and limp were enough for the police to call it. Aryn watched as two men left the car parked in front of hers and headed into the shop. They entered the shop and slowly approached the table. The two men drew weapons and started speaking to the man. He stood turned toward them and placed his hands on his head. The two men, clearly officers at this point, instructed him to lie on the ground before cuffing him. What the officers didn't see but Aryn did was Tina's smiling face as she looked toward the door.

Now, just a half block away, Charlie stepped into his car holding his hot cup of coffee. He grinned as he sipped it. A stroke of genius, really; he had called ahead and placed two separate orders. And then had offered a homeless man a scarf to keep him warm and a free cup of coffee. The only catch? To go and pick up the first order and have a seat by the window. Two people in line behind the vagrant stood Charlie, waiting patiently for his cup of coffee. He watched as the police made the man lie on the ground and waved goodbye to Tina with a wink.

"How in the hell did you guys screw this up?" Chance yelled at the officers. It was ridiculous to say, as he knew anybody would have, given all of the evidence. He was just so mad he was basically just letting some steam off. He paced the room in front of the officers, trying to cool off. The men nervously shifted their weight foot to foot and avoided his angry gaze.

After what seemed like an eternity to both of them, Chance stopped pacing and took a deep breath before apologizing. "Look, I am sorry. You did everything right. God!" He reached into his pockets searching for his phone. "Where is the guy now?"

The older of the two officers said they had him in holding. "Okay, try and get what you can from him, description-wise, and pull any CCTV in the area. See if we can get a visual of Charlie."

Before the men left, he yelled after them, "And bring me that coffee, girl!"

The youngest officer looked back and corrected him, "I think they like to be called baristas, Captain." Wide eyed, the older one grabbed him by the arm and pulled him out of sight of the now seething captain.

At the same time, in the hospital, Gershing had an unwelcome visitor. At first what he thought was a nurse soon became apparent that, in fact, was not. A voice whispered into his ear to be calm and everything would be all right. Too weak from the damage to his body and also because of the drugs that he had been administered, he was unable to resist. He was lowered into a wheelchair and pushed down the hall toward the elevator. The on-call nurse was too busy making rounds with the doctor to see any of this unfortunately, or he would have been able to stop what was surely to be a very bad day for Gershing.

Forty minutes after the officers left his office, Chance was straightening his tie in his office mirror. Sadly, he placed his dress cap on his head and checked to make sure all his awards were straight. As his fingers brushed over his award for bravery, he was reminded of Rashan pulling him to safety from a speeding car.

Merrings, Pullman, and Truman knocked gently on their new captain's door. He opened the door but said nothing as he joined them in walking down to the garage. It was going to be a hard day.

It was lunch when Aryn made it back to the office and checked her messages. As she listened to her answering machine, she was surprised yet again to hear Chance's voice. His request was simple yet seemed in sheer earnest. Checking her watch, she hung up and hurried back outside to her car.

A cold rain fell on the men's shoulders as they stood around the flag draped coffin of Rashan and the slightly smaller coffin of his wife beside him. Boys are taught from an early age not to cry, to be tough, to never show weakness. But sometimes it was more difficult to hold that reserve. They listened to the minister give the captain's eulogy. It was beautiful and truly showed how much Rashan affected those around him. While the captain's wife's was much shorter, it meant just as much. They had both become family to those that were in attendance. Chance felt so alone, burdened with more than he had ever had to bear before.

As the eulogy was ending, he felt a soft hand grasp his. He looked to see who it was and found himself looking into the comforting eyes of Aryn. She squeezed his hand and looked back at the caskets, as seven officers stepped forward to fire three volleys into the air with their rifles. As the last shot's echo faded, a tear escaped Chance's eye. Aryn reached out and brushed it from his cheek with her soft hand. Chance and his friends watched as the top of Rashan's casket disappeared into the grave and turned to leave, more resolute than ever to catch the old Captain's killer.

As Chance and his detectives were driving away, on the opposite side of Dayton, Tina was being asked to accompany the officers from earlier to the precinct. She nervously folded her green apron and carefully tucked it beneath the counter before following the men out to their squad car.

Gershing was in bad shape as he waited, against his will, in his abductor's trunk. He could hear the rain drops fall against the metal lid. With his sight gone, he felt like he was suffocating because of his lifelong battle with claustrophobia. Logically he knew that fresh air was getting in just fine from the interior of the car, but emotionally, he couldn't control his fear. His crippled hands feebly slapped the top of the trunk in hopes someone would rescue him. But the only person who did hear him was his returning tormentor. He heard them slam their fist against the hood in response and then the driver's side door slam shut. As the car drove away, he knew it was just a matter of time before whoever was driving the car would kill him.

Most of the day was uneventful for Charlie at the office. Small talk around the coffee maker was uninteresting as it usually was. He smiled and forced conversation with those around him, but his mind was consumed with Tina's smiling face. He sat at his desk, avoiding messaging her with every fiber of his being. For one thing, it would seem clingy; another, he didn't want to put her in jeopardy. But as the day wore on, he couldn't hold out anymore and he grabbed his phone from his desk drawer.

There was a message in Snapchat from Tina. He must have missed it because he had the phone on silent. It read, "The police want me to go to their station to ask me questions. I'm deleting Snapchat so they don't see that I have been talking to you."

Furious, Charlie grabbed his jacket from his cubicle wall and headed toward the door. They had involved someone he cared about; there was already enough of that going on from his "admirer." He had to do something about this.

In a cold room, Tina sat in a hard metal chair, waiting for someone to come in and ask her about her involvement with Charlie. The clock ticked loudly in the mostly bare room, making her more anxious with each passing second. She nervously rubbed her legs and tried to keep her face composed. The last thing she wanted to look like was guilty. She was surprised to see that there wasn't a two-way mirror in the room, like she had seen on TV. Instead, she found a camera in both corners of the room and a microphone on the table in front of her. Just when the ticking was almost too much to take, the door opened, and in walked Chance. "Good afternoon, Tina," He began.

As Chance began asking Tina questions, outside in the station, a desk sergeant was arguing with a man. After a heated debate, the desk sergeant stood and walked up to the interrogation room door and knocked. The door opened, and after a brief conversation, it closed again. The desk sergeant returned to his desk and nodded at the man he had been arguing with just a few minutes before. A brief moment later, Tina stepped out of the room confused, and Chance followed, pointing to the man still standing at the desk.

"Apparently, your lawyer wants to have a word with you before we begin." Tina nodded, hiding her confusion, as she approached the man from behind. Chance watched as she walked away, annoyed at the interruption but eventually turned away and went into the room to await her return. As she rounded the desk to face her savior, she had to stifle a shocked gasp when she saw his face. There in front of her was Charlie.

She grabbed his arm and pulled him away from the desk. "What are you doing here?" she whispered.

"I couldn't let you do this alone, not on my account," he whispered back.

She shook her head. "You have to get out of here! Hurry!" she demanded quietly.

"Okay, but first, I want you to tell them something very specific," he said, looking around to make sure no one could overhear them, then continued. She listened intently, nodded, shook his hand, and then walked back to the sergeant's desk to be escorted to the interrogation room.

Outside, Charlie took off his tie and stepped into his car to await Tina's release. He turned on the radio and his mind drifted. He was trying to decide what to do about Tammy. Tina and Aryn weren't the only ones in danger now. He had a plan to discover where they were being held, but all of the pieces of the puzzle had to fall perfectly into place for this to work. And unfortunately, it all hinged on another death. And the sooner, the better.

Somewhere in the night, Gershing's body fell heavily onto the cold, hard concrete. He could smell the dust on the floor and hear a woman's muffled pleas a short distance from him. He tried to crawl away from his captor, but a firm hand grabbed his ankles and tied them together. As he heard them walk away, slamming a heavy metal door, he tried to free himself but discovered he was tied to a metal post not more than three feet away. He laid there in pain and gurgled a wet moan from his deformed mouth. From his mouth ran a stream of drool, forming a small pool beneath his face. The drugs had started to wear off and the pain was overwhelming. His tear ducts now sutured, burned from the salty fluid threatening to escape from behind the stitches. He let out a sound that should have been sobbing but now sounded like a baying cow.

A satisfied smile reflected in the rearview mirror as Gershing's captor drove away into the night. One last chore to do.

Chapter 28

A Description of Terror

Tasha, a prostitute, could feel someone watching her. Having just been dropped off again after a liaison with a John, she straightened her sweatshirt and wiped her bright pink lipstick off with her hand. Finding her reflection in the lighted window of a local bar, she applied more lipstick and then flipped off the waitress who was shooing her away from the window. Proudly, she stomped her way back down the street. Finding a bench to sit on she pulled out her one-hitter and backed it with weed she carried in her backpack. She lit the end and leaned into the back of the bench, taking a deep pull off the opposite end as she did. It wasn't enough to affect her for very long, but the familiar smell eased her worries a bit. She watched the smoke curl away into the night and tried to forget what she just did for twenty dollars. It wasn't the stuff she did, really; it was the men she did it with. It was always some smelly old man or strung-out meth head. Not that she considered herself much better, but it still disgusted her. But the money was easy, when they actually paid her. Each dollar earned always seemed to be smoked away by the end of the night.

She hadn't always been this way. She went to college for a year until the cost got too high. Then her dad died and her mom couldn't hold a job because she was disabled. By the time she had moved back in, her mother was already doing sexual favors in order to have money to cover the pain medication. She tried to help, but every dollar she brought home from her job at a fast food restaurant her mother would use to buy more pills. Rent was never paid on time and food was scarce, so she turned to drinking to make it through the stresses of life. Then as things go, the drinking wasn't enough. Pills, turned to weed, weed into meth, meth into heroin, and before she knew it, she was doing the same thing as her mother to get her next fix.

She sighed and stood to walk to her corner again. She pulled her sweatshirt closer to her body as a snowflake fell in front of her eyes. She smiled a bit, remembering the magic of when she was a little girl seeing snow falling each year. But those days were far gone, and now she saw herself as flawed trash. She choked back a small cry and continued down the dark street. Behind her, the noise from the bar grew steadily quieter as she put more distance between them. Soon, the only sounds were occasional passing cars and the far-off sound of police sirens. She passed by a meth head loudly rambling angrily to herself about something unintelligible. It wasn't until she reached her corner that she settled back under a storefront overhang to avoid the falling snow. The streetlight flickered overhead, sending a foreboding atmosphere. She lit a cigarette and waited for her next customer. Unknown to her, she was being watched from a car just up the street.

A truck pulled up in front of her, and a man rolled down the window. She walked toward him and leaned into the window. Inside were three men, clearly drunk. "How much?" the driver asked.

"Forty for you, two hundred for all three," she told him. The three men looked at each other then laughed. Before she could react, the man grabbed her arm so she couldn't get away and poured a spit cup, full of tobacco and saliva, on her hair. She broke away and fell to the ground as the men pulled away, laughing and calling her a whore. She pulled herself to her feet and chased after them, cussing until she could no longer keep up.

Shaking she wiped her hair with her hands and tried to rinse some of it out in a puddle that had formed by the curb. Then she wiped her eyes and dragged her feet back under her overhang. She stared out into the snow, falling harder now, and cussed loudly. Lighting another cigarette, she failed to see the car door down the street open.

A voice called out to her, and she tried to see who the shadowy figure was in the distant snowfall. "You want to make some money?" She squinted but was able to make out what they looked like.

"Maybe. What for?" she yelled back. The figure beckoned for her to follow. She looked around; not seeing anyone, she shrugged and took another drag as she followed.

The figure entered an abandoned warehouse just around the corner. Many businesses had closed recently due to a pandemic forcing them to lay people off; this eventually led to their filing bankruptcy and abandoning their buildings. So when they stuck their head back out and gestured for her to go in, she didn't think too much about it. However, as she came closer and closer to the dimly lit doorway, she became warier. Something in the back of her head was screaming to walk away, but the pull of her next fix made her take step after step.

Once inside, she pulled off her hood and ran her fingers through her still tobacco and spit-covered hair. She wiped her hands on her sweatshirt and nervously walked toward her benefactor. Before she realized what was happening, she was stabbed with a syringe that was hidden in their hand. The plunger drove home, and a hot feeling flooded through her veins, and she broke free of their grip. She ran for the door, but her attacker was too quick and blocked her way. Turning away, she ran the opposite direction down a dark hallway. The broken windows allowed just enough moonlight in to allow her now addled mind to hallucinate demons reaching out for her. She screamed and threw herself to the ground, covering her head to protect herself. That would be her undoing, unfortunately.

She was suddenly jerked into a kneeling position by her hair, and a thin wire wrapped around her pretty neck. She struggled and managed to get three of her fingers behind the wire. The wire sliced into her fingers as she tried desperately to protect her neck. A knee drove into her back for leverage, and the wire cut through her carotid artery; blood sprayed onto the shadowed walls. She fell to the ground, clutching her neck, and her attacker watched as the young prostitute crawled away, a bloody trail behind.

They say regret is always the last thing you have before you go to the other side, but for the prostitute, it was her as a young girl staring up in wonder at that first snowflake. As her eyes lost their light, a hand brushed the hair off of her face and gently closed her eyes.

Chapter 29

The First Piece Falls into Place

The news that another prostitute was killed shocked the entire city. It had been weeks since the last one, and the police had seemed to be well on their way to catching Charlie. Newspapers and television headlines had Charlie's sketch at the forefront of every story.

Tina watched the headlines, oddly relieved. She now knew that Charlie was telling her the truth. He couldn't have been the one who was killing the women because he was still beside her, safely in bed sleeping. After picking her up, he offered to take her home and drop her off, which she readily agreed too, but when he pulled up in front of her apartment, she realized she didn't want to be left alone. She invited him inside. One thing led to another, and they soon found themselves wrapped in each other's arms. Passion filled the apartment. Each touch on one another's bodies sent sensations they had never experienced before all over them, ending in a crescendo of fireworks. They fell asleep beside each other's naked bodies, worn out from their loving tryst. The French call it the "little death," and so true it was.

She reached over and gently shook Charlie awake. He moaned as he stretched his body and looked up at her smiling face. "Another woman was killed last night. They are saying it was you again," she informed him and then pulled one of her long blond hairs off of his arm.

He shook his head to clear away the cobwebs and nodded. "I was hoping this would happen," he said. She didn't say anything but didn't look amused at his response. He noticed, so he explained further. "What I mean is, this needed to happen to start putting my plan into action. And added benefit, now you know I'm telling you the truth."

Tina agreed and waited for him to continue.

Charlie raised himself to a seated position and pulled the sheet up to cover his waist. "Now if the captain who interviewed you yesterday takes the hint you left him, I'll have the prostitute killer exactly where I need him."

Tina sighed and rolled out of bed. All of these chess moves were tiring. She pulled a robe around her shoulders and headed out of the room. Charlie watched her hips sway as she walked away. No longer in the mood to think about his plans, he jumped out of bed and chased after her. Down the hall, giggling floated through the air.

Chance sat in his office, still dark, and thought about what his next move should be. The morning shift was starting to take their positions in the precinct. He watched them as they received their briefings from the night shift. When the final night shift officer left the bullpen, he arose from his chair and opened the door. "Let me get all the detectives in the briefing room in fifteen minutes," he called out then turned and flipped his lights on before returning back to his desk to gather his notes together.

Chance walked into the briefing room and faced his detectives. "So here's where we are at with Charlie. Yesterday, I interviewed the barista from the coffee shop we believe that he frequented. She didn't tell us much, but she did say that the guy that the manager was speaking about works at a bar called Ned Peppers in the Oregon district downtown. She said he sometimes wears one of their employee shirts after his shift ends and believes that he may tend bar. I need a couple of undercovers to go there tonight. It can't be our regular crew because there is a good chance that Charlie knows what they look like."

Three hands raised at this request.

"Okay, great. Tom, Ivan, Matt, I want you to take one of our female detectives with you tonight. Expect to be there from when they open till they close. If you make him, I want you to call me before you move on him."

He stopped for a moment to make sure they understood and then continued. "The medical examiner's results came back on the prostitute from last night. No prints, no hair or blood. We have come up short again, but I want officers on the ground there again today to see if we missed anything. Pullman, I want you to head that up. Take along the feds—they have requested to look at the warehouse."

Pullman nodded.

"As I have been here since last night, I'm going to run home and catch a few hours' sleep, and I'll be back at noon to hear your status. It's going to be a long one today. I'm approving overtime today."

The men grimaced but said nothing as he walked out of the room. Pullman followed. "Hey, Captain, I just wanted to make sure about this before you left. Do you want me to call you if I find anything before I send it to the lab?" he asked.

"Yeah, I don't want anyone to know about this until we can get a handle on how Charlie is finding out about everything," Chance explained and then nodded goodbye and headed to his office to grab his coat.

When Chance finally made it home, he fell onto his couch, exhausted. He reached for the bottle of scotch on the coffee table, when a loud thump came from down the hall. He stood up quickly and drew his weapon. From the bedroom came Aryn's voice. "I'm sorry! That was me! I was just trying to clean up before I left for work."

He sighed and put his gun back in his holster before she came out. "What are you doing here?" he asked.

"Well, you said we were going to have dinner last night, but you never showed, so I thought maybe I would surprise you when you made it home, but you never came," she called back before she came into the living room and threw her arms around his neck.

He frowned. "You're right! I'm sorry, I forgot all about it. Another girl was killed last night, and I ended up working all night.

I should have called, but I got wrapped up in the investigation," he explained.

"Don't worry about it!" she said, smiling. "I figured it was something like that. So any leads?"

He shook his head. "No, the body was clean. I have the guys looking the warehouse back over again, but I don't think anything will turn up. But…" he trailed off.

"But what?" she asked.

"We have a witness that says that Charlie works at a bar in the Oregon district. We are looking into it tonight," he finished.

She nodded and then asked, "Does that mean that you're working again tonight?"

He said no, explaining that the detectives would call if they found anything.

She nodded, understanding, and then said, "Good! Let me make you dinner tonight!"

He smiled, agreed, and then kissed her.

"Have a great day at work, baby. I'm going to go lie down for a bit before I head back in. Dinner at eight?"

"Let's make it nine. I have an article to turn in before it gets sent out in the morning," she said as she grabbed her purse and closed the door behind her. He smiled and kicked off his shoes; within minutes, he was asleep.

It seemed like he wasn't asleep for more than a few minutes before his alarm went off at noon. He sat up slowly, stretched, and rubbed his tired eyes. He pulled on his shoes and then stood in front of the mirror to straighten his uniform. The tired, aged face that looked back was foreign to him. His eyes were red and strained. He leaned back and put eye drops into them and then blinked several times. Grabbing his electric razor, he headed out the door and back toward the office.

When he arrived, the precinct was abuzz. "Captain. Captain!" Merrings called out to him.

Chance made his way through the maze of desks and stood in front of him.

"Hey, Captain. I just got off the phone with Ned Peppers. They have a bartender there that fits the description, and his name is Charles Turner. He starts his shift at seven tonight."

Chance nodded enthusiastically and then stopped. "You didn't tell them you were with the police, right?" he asked.

"No. I told them I was a reporter, looking to interview the staff about how they were feeling a year after that lunatic shot up their bar last year. I told them I was looking to talk to a bartender I met a week ago and gave them Charlie's description."

Chance nodded in approval. "Nice! Okay, I want you to go there and wait outside tonight with Truman in case the plainclothes need backup. Don't go in unless they need help, though. I'm hoping we can keep him on surveillance without him realizing it. I don't want him getting away on some technicality in court."

Merrings said okay and headed toward Truman's desk to let him know the plan, and Chance headed back to his office. It was going to be a long day.

Chapter 30

The Day Prior

Unknown to everyone except Charlie himself, he had made a quick search of different bars websites in the Oregon district. It didn't take long to search through photos and staff names to track down a some-what believable doppelganger that fit his description. Then it was just a matter of telling Tina to drop this information on Chance's lap. He knew that Chance would let her go if he thought she was being helpful, and with the police busy at Ned Peppers, he would have some more room to track down his admirer.

So far, everything was falling into place. But there were a few more things he had to square away before he could call it a night. As he waited for Tina to leave the station, he placed another call, this time to a familiar face. As he spoke, the person on the other end listened intently without speaking. When he finished, he hung up the phone.

On the other end of that phone call sat Aryn. Shocked that she had received a phone call from Charlie himself; she sat there listening unable to form the words she was searching for. Just as she had pulled herself together enough to ask a question, he hung up. She looked at the receiver; the number was unlisted. She sat there in stunned silence as she reviewed what he had just revealed to her. She reached again for her phone to call Chance but then thought better of it. What Charlie said needed to get into the paper post haste. She opened a new word file and started typing furiously.

Charlie looked out the window to see if Tina had made it free yet. Alas, that was not the case, so he turned back to screen on his phone again. After a few minutes, he found what he was looking for and started filling out a form on his phone. He had just finished with everything when Tina came out and knocked on the passenger side window. He reached over and unlocked the door, allowing her to get in. She sat there for a few moments in silence and then laid her head on his shoulder. He said nothing and just stroked her hair. She eventually raised her head and asked him to drive her home.

As the car pulled away, she began telling him everything that had happened inside the police station.

Chapter 31

The Following Night

Merrings and Truman pulled up in front of Ned Peppers at a quarter to six and settled in for a long night. The back seat was filled with surveillance electronics and cameras. They watched the crowd shuffle past the bar on their way to their homes. "Think we will get lucky tonight?" Merrings asked.

"Maybe," Truman shrugged.

"I thought we had him at the coffee shop, but…"

Merrings nodded in agreement. "Yeah. Charlie's smart, no doubt about it."

They spent their time waiting for their suspect to arrive in silence. They were long practiced at these sorts of things. Between them they had probably over five hundred hours on different stake-outs. When one would need to urinate, he would use a bottle and then put it behind them on the floor of the car. Luckily, they were practiced enough to dehydrate themselves before they did this sort of thing, so it didn't happen too often. Merrings took his turn watching the door while Truman closed his eyes for a bit. Before Truman had fallen asleep, however, he was nudged by his partner.

"That's our guy," Merrings indicated by pointing his finger at an athletic middle-aged blond man entering the front door. Truman called into the precinct on his phone, in order to avoid someone listening into the police scanner, and let Chance know that the man had arrived.

Chance hung up the phone and called out to the officers who had volunteered earlier. "Go get changed, your guy just showed up at Ned Peppers." Four officers stood from behind their desks and headed to the locker room. Satisfied, Chance looked at his watch. Unable to think of what else he could do now, he grabbed his jacket to head home. It would only be a little bit longer, and he would be able to enjoy a dinner with Aryn.

It was around seven thirty when Truman and Merrings saw the officers head into the bar. There was nothing to do now but wait for some sort of signal, if they were needed. "You want to order some food?" Merrings asked.

"Uh...yeah. Might as well. DoorDash?" Truman said as he picked up his phone to place an order. About twenty-five minutes later, they had a knock on their car window. They tipped the man, and he thanked them and headed away. The men devoured the burgers while they watched TV on Merrings's phone he had set up on the dash. Before they realized it, they had both passed out.

As Charlie drove away from the two detectives, he took off his DoorDash hat and placed it back inside of his book bag. He mused at how easy it was to get a job online under an assumed name. Not to mention how quickly Amazon could deliver uniforms. He reached into his pocket and removed the tranquilizers from his pocket and tossed them into the bag as well. If he hurried, he could still meet up with Tina for dinner.

The desk sergeant answered the phone, listened intently, and then said goodbye. He hesitated, trying whom to best tell about the call he just received. After a moment, he dialed Detective Pullman's cell phone. "Detective? This is Sergeant Siler. I just got a call from the hospital. They can't find Gershing. They reviewed the video, and it looks like someone came in, put him in a wheelchair, and rolled him out the door. I'm having them send the video over."

Pullman told the man thank you and hung up the phone. He sighed and turned back to useless search at the warehouse where the young woman was just killed.

Chance stood in the shower, letting the heat melt away his sore muscles. The steam was doing its best to clear out his sinuses from the day's city smog. Finished, he stepped out and wiped the fog from the mirror before toweling off and combing his hair. Dressed in a pair of khakis and a tight-fitting polo, he slid on his loafers and headed to the bed room to apply a small amount of cologne to his wrists and neck. It would be just a little bit longer before he would meet with Aryn for dinner. He grabbed his carry pistol and put it in its shoulder holster before putting both the holster and a sports jacket on. Looking approvingly at himself in the mirror, he shut off the lights and closed the door behind him.

He found Aryn looking through the menu at Giordano's, a city favorite when it came to Italian cuisine. She bent down and kissed her cheek before sitting across from her. "Hi! How was work?" she asked.

"Pretty good, pretty good," he said with a smile. "I think we're about to be done with all of this."

She let a reluctant smile escape but then broke the news that Charlie had called her.

He shifted in his chair and lowered his voice. Gruffly, he asked her why she hadn't called him immediately. She sheepishly hid her eyes from him and said nothing. "Damn it, Aryn!" he said. "What did he say?"

"He said that wasn't the one who killed those girls and that someone was doing it and blaming it on him," she quietly told him.

"Did he give you any proof?" he asked incredulously.

"He said that all the proof we would need would be at the top floor of the Stratacache Tower next Saturday night."

Chance looked at her trembling and instantly regretted being so tough on her. "Okay. I'm guessing you're running the story tomorrow?"

She nodded.

"All right, I need you to leave out the part about Stratacache Tower," he said and rested his hand on hers. She smiled again and agreed.

Their meal was eaten in silence, not because of what had happened between them but because the food was so good they just sat there enjoying it together. After dinner, they talked about everything that had been happening in their lives over a glass of red wine. He spoke of his reluctance in being the new captain, and she spoke about her deadlines and stories she was being assigned. By the end of the night, they were more than okay. She kissed him passionately on the lips and made plans to spend the weekend with him before saying goodbye.

When he finally made it home, he made sure to place the phone next to his head to ensure he wouldn't miss the inevitable call from Merrings before nodding off to sleep—a call that would never come.

Chapter 32

One Man Gone

Chance buried his head in his hands, trying to hide his despair and annoyance. Everything had gone wrong last night at Ned Peppers. Merrings and Truman were in the hospital getting checked out that they were okay after their drugging last night, and Charles left the bar after it closed. Because the two detectives were asleep, no one followed him. To top it all off, when uniformed police officers went to his apartment this morning, his roommate informed him that he hadn't made it home last night and had no idea where he was. They had let Charlie slip through their fingers again! Now he had found out Gershing had been taken out of the hospital. Things just kept getting worse.

While he waited to find out the status of his two detectives, a warrant was waiting for approval from the court. When that came through, they would be able to search Charlie's apartment. Chance lifted his head and ran his fingers through his hair. What was he going to do now? His suspect was in the wind, and it would just be a matter of time before he killed again.

His phone rang loudly, and he grabbed at it quickly. He listened intently to the other end, and after a brief conversation, he hung up the phone. Merrings and Truman were given clearance to return to work. Apparently, whatever drug they were given was relatively safe, a type of drug called Propofol that is used to keep patients asleep who need a ventilator. Chance walked out of the office and checked the fax machine for a signed warrant. Nothing yet. Now all he could do was wait for the detectives to join him.

An hour later, Merrings and Truman, looking quite haggard, sat facing the captain. "How are you guys doing?" The detectives shrugged, embarrassed.

"Look, stuff happens. We have to move past this and figure out what we can do now," Chance said reassuringly.

Merrings looked at his partner and then back at Chance. "I've been trying to remember what the delivery guy looked like, but I haven't been able to, and I tried calling GrubHub, and they gave me the guy's full name and address, but it ended up being a fake."

Chance nodded; he expected nothing less of Charlie. "But if Charlie was inside the whole time, then he has a partner, right?"

It was Truman's turn to talk. "That's what we figure. The only thing I can't figure out is how he knew we were going to even be there or that we were on to him at all."

Chance stood and grabbed his empty mug off his desk. He walked to the coffee pot and poured himself a cup of coffee and then returned to his desk. "Okay. If you guys are good for the day, I want you to take a team over to Charles's place and check for clues there. Pullman and the agents didn't come up with anything either at the warehouse, so we are just spinning our wheels on all fronts. I'm meeting with the feds later to start planning our sting on Stratacache Tower next Saturday." Merrings nodded and left with Truman in tow.

"Good afternoon. I'm Detective Merrings, and this is Detective Truman from the Dayton PD, we are here to serve a warrant on this apartment," he said as he showed the warrant to Charlie's roommate.

"Um, yeah, sure," the stunned roommate said as he opened the door the rest of the way and stepped out of the way. Truman thanked him as passed. The police began sweeping the apartment in hopes of finding a hiding Charlie. No such luck was to be had so they began searching through his bedroom.

While the uniformed officers were busy, Merrings and Truman turned their attention to questioning his roommate. "How long have you known Charles?"

"About thirteen months," the man said.

"Has he ever done anything that would strike you as odd behavior?"

The man thought for a minute and then said, "Um, I guess he talks about sex a lot."

The detectives nodded and then Truman asked, "By talking about sex, what do you mean?"

"Well, I'm gay, so I guess I don't understand straight men, but it seemed like he would fit sex into every topic we talked about. Which was weird because I don't think he ever brought a girl home with him. Oh! And he watched porn *a lot*!"

Truman nodded. "How do you know he watched porn a lot?"

The man laughed sarcastically and explained, "You could hear it playing through the walls, like all the time!"

As if on cue, an officer came out and handed Merrings a box in gloved hands. Merrings opened the lid and then closed it quickly. Avoiding locking eyes with Charlie's roommate, he handed Truman the box. Truman opened the lid. "Son of a bitch!"

Back in the precinct, the warrant team was laying out the evidence from Charlie's apartment on the briefing room table, when Chance walked in. "What did we find?" he asked.

Merrings, sitting in the corner, pointed toward the box in the center of the table. Chance walked over and lifted the lid off the shoe box. Inside, hundreds of nude photos of underage girls were piled on top of each other. Chance bowed his head and closed the lid again.

"So he's a pedophile," he said to no one in particular.

Merrings nodded and then joined Truman at the table. Grabbing an evidence bag, he opened it and poured the contents out onto a plastic sheet. He then grabbed a UV light and shined it over top of a small skirt; there bright as day was semen. Chance looked up at the ceiling and placed his hands on his hips.

"Okay. Process this at the lab, and see if we can find out who's little girl's skirt this belongs to. Did the roommate have anything to add?"

Truman shook his head, but then added, "The only thing he said was that he was surprised that he didn't come home last night because he keeps antipsychotic medication there that he regularly takes." With that, Chance left the room and went to his office.

Chapter 33

Enlèvement

As much as he tried, he couldn't get his calls through to Aryn. The phone would ring and ring, ending with him leaving another message. After a few hours, he made a call to her office to see if she had made it on that day. They said she hadn't. Worried, Chance sent one final text and tried to focus on the investigation at hand. It wouldn't be long before Tom and Turtle would be joining him to figure out the best approach for next Saturday.

Chance opened his door and asked Merrings if they had written their report yet. Truman stuck his thumb up from Merrings's side. "Thanks, send it to my email please," Chance said and closed his door again. He sat down again and refreshed his screen. He wanted to make sure he had everything laid out for the agents when they came, so they had everything he had. If they wanted to catch Charlie, it was going to take everyone working in perfect sync. Seeing that the report had made it through, he sent it to the printer. He grabbed it on the way to the briefing room and asked a uniformed officer to bring the evidence bags from Charles's apartment up from the evidence room. Then he laid out everything across the table to give Turtle the best picture they could. They needed him to make the most accurate analysis of Charlie yet.

An hour later, Tom and Turtle joined him in the briefing room. Chance filled them on everything that had occurred the night before and that morning. They listened intently and looked over Merrings's report. "I find it interesting that Charlie has child pornography," Turtle said while rubbing his chin. "I suppose it's not unheard of that serial killers have a sorted past with sex. John Wayne Gacy and David Berkowitz both had a collection of child pornography when they were caught. It just surprises me that with Charlie's high moral code that he would personally have a vice like this."

He put down the report and put on a pair of gloves, before shuffling through the rest of the evidence bags. "The report said there was a skirt?" Chance nodded and told him that it was being processed in the lab.

"Were there any weapons or any sort of collection that would indicate trophies that he would have collected from his victims?" Turtle asked.

Chance answered, "No. Nothing."

Tom, who was on the other side of the table, spoke up. "That's weird. I don't think I've ever worked one of these cases where there weren't trophies of some sort. Women's hair, bones, jewelry—serial killers get their kicks out of revisiting their handiwork."

Both men asked to have time with the evidence to complete their reports. Chance agreed and asked them to join him when they were done. Chance closed the door behind him and surveyed the precinct. Merrings and Truman were still at their desks typing away at their computer keyboards. He walked over and rested his hands on their shoulders. "Why don't both of you call it a day? Go home and get some rest. I'll call you if I need you. Just be back tomorrow first thing." Truman looked at him with tired eyes, appreciably.

Alone in his office again, he tried and failed to get a hold of Aryn again. *Where could she be?* he wondered aloud. Trying to shake the growing concern he had for Aryn, he searched through Stratacache Tower's website for contact information. Finding what he was looking for, he placed a call to the building manager. He explained that he was with the police department and what was going on, after which, he requested the building plans be sent to his fax machine. Satisfied that the man was more than willing to help, he said he would be in touch with him again soon and to keep it quiet.

The agents joined him as he was looking over the tower's building plans. "What do you have there?" Tom asked of the captain.

"I'm trying to decide how we can best watch the building for Charlie," he explained.

Tom nodded and looked over his shoulder at the papers. After a moment, he pointed at various areas of the top floor. "We can place hidden cameras in these corners and have a full view of the entire floor. And if we place unmarked vehicles outside, we can watch all of the entrances to make sure no one enters. We can put them out there Friday night so Charlie doesn't see them pull up."

He suggested. Chance agreed. They couldn't risk being caught again. "I'll put out a general order that the people watching the doors bring their food with them, so we don't run into the same issue as last night."

"So what did you find?" Chance asked the two men.

"Well, I believe I have enough, based on the evidence, to alter Charlie's profile. Charlie is more than likely a drug or alcohol user. More than likely has tattoos and/or body piercings, perhaps hidden by clothing. Possibly molested as a child by an older male adult he was familiar with, possibly a father, or a teacher. He more than likely has a caffeine addiction, which coincides with his morning coffee runs. Both of his parents are likely separated, at an early age, would be my guess. Of course, all of this is based solely on the evidence in that room," Turtle finished.

Chance thought about what Turtle had said for a moment. But then a thought occurred to him, so he voiced it, "I wonder if anyone has tried to get a hold of Charlie's parents yet." Sticking his head out of the office door, he yelled out to Pullman to look them up. Pullman waved in acknowledgment.

"We need to get online and make a call back to the head office. Is there a room we can use?" Tom asked when Chance had sat down again.

"Yeah, go ahead and use my office. I'm going to grab dinner anyways," he said and stood to leave. Turtle and Tom waved goodbye as the door closed behind him.

Chance drove out of the parking lot and turned south toward the newspaper's building. On his way, he tried to get a hold of Aryn again. Unsuccessful, he hung up and tried checking her Snapchat map function to see if she had enabled it, something he absolutely despised doing. Unfortunately, she had not. He laid his phone on the passenger seat and shuffled through his radio stations, trying to find some music to soothe his nerves. Normally, he wouldn't be this worried, but with everything going on and Charlie knowing who she was, it left her in constant danger.

Chance pulled into the parking lot and surveyed it. Not seeing her car, he turned around and headed toward her apartment. As he pulled up, he held his breath. Her car was nowhere to be seen.

Chapter 34

A Shadow in the Dark

From the cold floor, Gershing could just barely make out the muffled screams of a woman. He struggled to twist his deformed body toward the sounds, but it left him wheezing in pain, now that his pain medication had completely worn off. The girl, clearly gagged, screamed as best she could for help, but no one was coming. His eye sockets ached from the dryness. Slowly inching his body back toward the beam he was secured to, he felt for it with his head. After what seemed like forever, he felt the cold metal on the top of his head. He forced himself to sit up and lean against it for support.

Behind him, just up the hall, a door shut quietly. In front of it now stood a dark, shadowy figure. They stood there listening to the cries of the woman, until finally, the figure started toward her. As the figure approached, the cries grew louder and more feverish. Frantic, the woman strained against the ropes binding her and tears fell to the floor.

Gershing listened to her screams until suddenly, violently, they ceased completely. He took a gargled breath and held it, straining his one good ear to listen. Footsteps approached, and he began to sweat. He moaned in pain as a hand grabbed at his collar and dragged him back to the center of the room. Letting go, the figure walked away, humming.

Just twenty minutes to the south, Chance was searching in vain to find his lost love, Aryn. He looked through her windows, after not getting an answer to his knocks, no lights or movement was detectable inside. He sighed and walked back to his car. Nothing he tried seemed to be leading anywhere. It was still far too soon to put in a missing person's report, but being the captain must have some perks, right? He walked back to his car and turning on the radio he requested an APB, or all-points bulletin, for Aryn. He described her in detail and waited to hear the dispatcher and place it on the radio. Seeing nothing else he could do, he headed to his apartment to drink away his sorrows.

Charlie watched from down the street from Aryn's apartment with interest. He hadn't seen Chance this frantic yet. He smirked but empathized; it must be hell on him worrying that someone had taken her. Loud raps came from his trunk. Annoyed, he stepped out of his car and walked to the rear of the car. Opening the trunk, he slapped away the hands that flung outward toward him. He calmly but firmly threatened to shut them up for good, if there was any more noise. Assured, this wouldn't happen again, he closed the trunk lid and got back in his car. Seeing that Chance had already left, he turned his car toward downtown. When he arrived at his destination, he looked up at the tower looming overhead and then pulled into the parking garage. It wouldn't be much longer now, he thought and smiled to himself.

Alone in her apartment, Tina wrestled with her own personal demons. Was what Charlie was doing morally right? She knew that it was illegal, of course, but he was performing a service to the community in some ways, much like the police. Of course, she knew she was justifying his actions, but in some ways, she could see where he was coming from. She had been on the receiving end of evil before, and it was never rectified by the police. It was still out there, terrifying others. She buried her head in her pillow and cried. She felt so alone right then. She was in love with Charlie, like she had never been in love before. It was passionate, warm, familiar, it was everything she read about in romance novels. But right at the second, without him beside her, she felt alone and confused. She worried constantly that he would be caught and held her breath till he returned to her arms.

She turned onto her back and took a deep breath. It wasn't going to be much longer until this was all over.

Tom and Turtle closed their team's conversation with Washington. Their conversation had been extensive and exhausting, but now, all their bosses were as up to date as was humanly possible. "Want to grab dinner at Chili's?" Tom asked.

Turtle shrugged and said, "I feel like we eat there every night, but I guess that's okay." Tom nodded—he agreed—but being unfamiliar with the area still it was the easiest to find as it was just a block from their hotel. "You know, I forgot to send headquarters the evidence reports. Let me stop and get those faxed over before we leave." Turtle agreed and grabbed his coat off the back of his chair. "Okay, I'll be outside smoking."

Tom grabbed the reports and headed to the fax machine. There, sitting on top of the machine, was Aryn's APB. Tom read it quietly to himself as the report was being scanned in. When the report was finished, he placed the APB back on top. He mulled on this development as he wrapped his coat around his shoulders. He wondered why Chance had neglected to inform them. He was still thinking about this as he joined Turtle by the car. He updated Turtle while he smoked. Turtle leaned against the car in thought. Was it possible that Charlie had her? Absolutely, but something seemed off about that. "Did it say how long she's been missing?" he asked.

Tom shook his head but remained silent.

"This doesn't sound like Charlie if I am being honest. So far, he was just using her to send a message. If he took her, who would he be sending a message to, Chance? He always just writes a letter if he wants to do that," Turtle finished.

Tom agreed and said, "I think we need to make a pit stop before we eat."

Chapter 35

The Pit Stop

Tina heard a knock at her door. She smiled and hopped to her feet. Her little feet almost flew over the carpet in her haste to get to the front door. She expected Charlie's familiar face when she flung open the door, but instead she was greeted with two badges and a pair of very official-looking men. "Good evening, ma'am. I'm Agent Black, and this is Agent Tuttle with the FBI. We are working with the Dayton PD on a case. We have a few questions for you if that's all right." Her heart dropped into her stomach, and she nervously ushered them in.

"What, uh, what do you want?" she asked, trying to gather herself together.

"Well, ma'am, we are investigating a missing person. We just want to know if you have had any contact with the man who calls himself Charlie since you came down to the station?" he asked and watched for her reaction. She steeled herself and, as calmly as possible, shook her head. Turtle watched with interest.

Tom continued, "Well, there was a young lady who we believe may have been taken by him earlier today. Her name is Aryn, and she works at the *Dayton Daily*. Has the man you believe to be Charlie ever made mention of anybody by that name?"

This time, Tina was quite sure of herself. "No, I don't ever remember him saying anything like that," she said matter-of-factly.

Again, Turtle watched quietly. Tom let an awkward silence ensue before saying thank you. Turtle stood with him and followed her toward the door. Saying their polite goodbyes, they turned toward the street to leave, but just as the door was closing, Turtle turned and caught the door with his hand. "Really quick, and I apologize, can I use the bathroom really quickly? It's quite a drive to our hotel, and I'm not sure I'm going to make it." He laughed. She hesitated but then reluctantly agreed. Tom waited outside while his partner went in. A few minutes later, Turtle rejoined them and politely thanked her.

Tina watched them leave and took a deep sigh of relief. The buzzards were circling. And now she was even more involved than she ever thought she would be. She drew the curtains and fell to the couch and sobbed. Large tears fell down her beautiful cheeks and she shook as her nerves gave out.

Turtle chuckled out loud and leaned his head back onto the headrest. "What are you laughing at?" Tom asked.

"Well, she's definitely not always alone there," Turtle said.

"She has a man's toothbrush in her bathroom." Tom smiled.

"You sly son of a bitch." Turtle laughed, louder this time, and looked out the window. "We will have some of the detectives keep an eye on the place, starting tomorrow. Maybe we will get lucky," Tom said.

Just down the street, Charlie sat, cursing under his breath, in his car and watched the men drive away. He only had a little time before they had someone start watching Tina again. He sighed and pulled around the block and parked his car. He climbed a fence and went through the backyard to enter the rear of her apartment. Inside, he found Tina's shaking body on the couch. He reached down and rubbed her shoulders. "They're gone, they're gone," he said soothingly.

She looked up at his eyes and suddenly felt a little better. "You... you didn't kidnap a girl, did you?" She sniffled.

Chapter 36

Sunrise on a Snowy Street

Dawn came slowly creeping over the city skyline, revealing a heavy blanket of white fresh snow covering the streets. Chance's breath fogged the window as he drank his coffee and stared out into the morning light. He had heard nothing from Aryn the entire night, and nothing had come back on the APB. His nerves were strained, and his eyes were bloodshot. Rest had not come easy that night.

His cell phone rang, and hastily, he struggled to free it from his pocket. Alas, it was Tom, not who he was hoping it might be. "Captain?" Tom's disembodied voice asked.

"Yeah? What's up?"

Tom went on to explain everything that had happened the night before and asked what Chance wanted to do. "I'll have two unmarked vehicles parked on the street to watch the house. What did the boys in Washington have to say about everything?" Chance asked.

"They like our plan for Saturday, but they want to send up a team to set up surveillance cameras in the room. Also, they were going to bring in a drone to watch from the roof. Not sure if they want to have a few more of our agents on the ground yet, but they will be sending over a detailed plan of action by the end of the day." Chance thanked him and hung up the phone.

Finished with his call, he went into the bathroom to begin his morning routine. He turned on the shower and left to lay his uniform out on the bed. When he returned, he began shaving his masculine jawline free of the night's stubble. As the steam built up on the mirror, words appeared! He dropped his razor into the sink and backed away in shock. There in the steamy mirror was the word HELP! Chance took a photo with his phone called for a forensics team to meet him at his apartment then quickly showered and got dressed in anticipation of their arrival.

When the team arrived, with Pullman and Truman in tow, Chance let them in and showed the detectives the photo. "When was the last time Aryn has been here that you know of?" they asked.

"Well, it's been a few days. I'm pretty sure it was Tuesday," he explained.

"I'm sorry I have to ask this, but were you two intimate that evening?" Truman nervously asked. Chance knew that they had to ask but was still somewhat uncomfortable with answering. Still, he nodded. "Okay, where? At the bedroom?" Truman followed up. Again, Chance nodded and pointed down the hall.

The detectives headed away down toward the bedroom, while the forensics team started setting up for their testing of the bathroom. Chance watched them buzzing about from the kitchen and tried to steal his nerves while drinking another cup of coffee. The sounds of cameras and faint black light crept through the hallway. Everywhere, men were using brushes, looking for fingerprints. While he had witnessed the hectic blur of the forensics team working a hundred times before, he could now see how overwhelming it could be for the families that witnessed it happening in their own homes. It was almost like it was no longer his home.

The two detectives rejoined him. "I saw the APB last night. The reports said there wasn't anything yet. Has anybody said when they saw her last?" Pullman asked. Chance gloomily said that they had not.

"Okay, well, this is going to take a while. Did you want to head into the office and give these boys a chance to do their work?" he asked the forlorn captain. Chance put his hands in his pockets and agreed. There wasn't anything he could do here to help right now. The best thing he could do was head in and await the results.

"Okay, I'll ride back with you if that's alright? Truman is going to hang back and get back to us when it's all done." Nodding good-bye to Truman, Pullman followed Chance to his car.

On the ride to the station, the two spoke about everything that had happened with Aryn since Charlie's gift had arrived. Deep down, Pullman was just as worried about Aryn, but in hopes of calming his friend, he told him that he was sure that she was all right. Chance said nothing but doubted that this was true.

Pulling into his assigned parking spot, two men sat in silence for a moment. Pullman watched his friend; he had never witnessed his friend so broken before. The stress of everything recently had had a major effect on the man. His temples had started to gray, and his usual laugh lines that surround his crystal blue eyes had deepened and not from laughing. Chance rubbed his strained neck and swallowed the growing terror rising into his throat. Pushing open his car door, he stopped for a second, and without looking back at his friend, he said, "I had just said I loved her for the first time Tuesday, and now…" trailing off. Then he pulled his six-foot frame out of the car and headed toward the elevator, with Pullman close behind.

Inside the bullpen was louder than usual. People were scurrying about this way and that, trying to piece together where Aryn may have disappeared to. While no one had any proof as of yet, the general theory was that Charlie had taken her, leaving it extremely important to locate her. When a person disappeared, the first forty-eight hours were critical, mainly because that was the best time to follow up on leads. People's memories fade after that point on in detail. And while children were usually killed within three hours of being taken, adults statistically are killed within two days.

Chance and Pullman joined the two FBI agents, who were waiting for them in the briefing room. On the table was a box of Bills Donuts. Pullman eagerly searched the box for a cinnamon twist. Finding two, he poured himself a cup of coffee and joined them at the table.

He listened as Chance told the two agents about the message in the mirror. Turtle was the first to speak. "Can I see the photo that you took?" He looked at the photo with interest and then showed it to Tom. "Do you see the handwriting here?" he asked of Tom. Tom looked closer but didn't see what Turtle's point was. Seeing that Tom was not understanding he turned it back to Chance to make his point clear.

"The letters are written almost casually, like there isn't any haste in them. When someone is stressed and hurrying, the letters edges are sharp and have short ends, but these letters are very rounded and carefully written." Chance looked closer at the photo. The letters were very rounded. He wasn't at the education level that the doctor was, but Turtle was so self-assured that Chance suddenly felt a bit better.

"So... What you're saying is that she might not have been in trouble when she wrote this? But why would she have written the word at all then?" Chance asked, confused at the prospect.

"I couldn't say. I'm just saying that the handwriting indicates that there isn't stress involved when it was written," Turtle explained. The captain took back the phone and handed it to Pullman. "Have this sent to the lab to get printed off. I want our boys to see if they get the same thing that the Doctor here is seeing." Pullman reached for the phone and headed out to get the lab to have a look at it.

Chance leaned back in his chair and crossed his arms on his chest. "Okay, well…has Washington sent over their plan or are we still waiting on that?"

"Not yet, we aren't expecting anything until this evening, but that would still give us three days to get everything in place," Tom said.

"I'll have Truman send over what he gets from my apartment when he's done. In the meantime, let's get a few guys on Ms. Tina's place," Chance decided and stood to leave. Turtle and Tom stood with him and followed him out of the briefing room.

His once warm and inviting office now seemed dark and hollow in his depression. Everything was going wrong, and the snow outside added to his mood. Never one to suffer from seasonal affective disorder, his now strained emotions were becoming susceptible to it. Although the police station was well-heated, he shivered a bit as he sat down. He turned and looked at his wall of evidence he collected from Charlie's case. Somewhere, Aryn could be at Charlie's whims, and he was going to find her before it was too late.

An hour passed before the two unmarked vehicles pulled down the street from Tina's house. Settling in, they waited for some sign of life from the apartment. But none would come.

Tina cuddled with Charlie in his mahogany sleigh bed. She was warm and happy. Charlie had asked if she wanted to stay with him for a bit, and she timidly agreed at first. But when she walked into his house, it wasn't anything like she pictured it would be. From movies and television programs, she half-expected to see chains on the walls and skin-covered lampshades. The fact that it was very clean, well-organized, and very comfortable was a delightful surprise.

Charlie groaned as he stretched, then turned toward Tina. She ran her hand through the hair on his chest and almost purred. Charlie, suddenly very aware of the fact that he was naked, pulled the sheet more securely around his waist. She smiled and buried her head in his shoulder. Last night was amazing, as it usually was. A more generous lover she had never had. Chance rested his cheek on her hair and said, "What do you want for breakfast, princess?"

She shrugged, as she was not one who usually ate breakfast. "Maybe just some coffee." He brushed the hair away from her eyes and leaned in for a kiss before sitting up. She watched his lithe body as he walked to the kitchen. A few minutes later, she could hear the coffee maker gurgling, and it wasn't long before she could smell the rich aroma of coffee beans in the air. He came back into the room when it was complete and handed her a warm mug. She sat up, letting the sheet fall to her waist. He watched in fascination as she drank her coffee with no shame at her nakedness. Overcome with attraction, he took her cup and set it on the nightstand, and they both gave into their passion.

Chapter 37

The Setup

Two days had passed and Chance had still heard nothing of his missing love. Aryn had somehow disappeared off the face of the planet with no leads other than a cry for help written onto a mirror. Nothing else had been found in the apartment. No fingerprints that didn't belong there, no foreign hair, nothing. And it still didn't explain why she would have been there without him.

Chance crumpled a copy of the report and threw it into the wastebasket by his desk. It would be just a few minutes until he was to join the task force in the briefing room, and he had nothing new to give them. The night before, a task force sent from the FBI headquarters arrived. Their vans were parked in a remote location, and they arrived in small two-man groups at intervals to avoid drawing any attention to their being in the area. As of now, they were all gathered in the briefing room and getting a quick update from both Turtle and Tom. He watched through the window opposite the bullpen and readied himself to answer any questions they may have. Finally finding nothing else he could do, he begrudgingly stood up and headed across the bullpen.

The agents turned their heads and watched the captain enter. He motioned for the agents to continue and took his place at the end of the table. Tom continued talking. "As you can see, the top floor is surrounded on 70 percent of its walls by windows, so seeing everything from the outside should not be a problem. We are planning on placing snipers on buildings opposite it. We are not sure as of now whether or not Charlie has been up there as of late, so we have to assume he is aware of what is in the room, adding furniture or removing some could alert him that someone is watching. The tech team of course has the final say. However, our current recommendation is to place cameras in these locations," he finished while pointing at various locations on a blueprint projected onto the wall.

The tech team began discussing among themselves until one of them spoke up. "We think the locations are fine, but we would like to set up on the roof and control two drones from above. It will give us heat signatures and a good view of its surroundings."

Tom nodded and added, "Okay, we will check with the FAA and make sure we are good for that air space, but that's still pretty low, so as long as we don't go crazy, we should be fine."

Turtle stood and introduced Chance. "Gentlemen, this is Captain Roning. His team will be working in tandem with us on this operation." Chance stood and forced a smile. "Good morning. I have been working on this case from the beginning, both as a detective and as the captain, if there are any questions I can try and answer them now."

The men were courteous, but it was apparent to the young captain that they weren't interested in his insight on this case. Just as he was about to sit down again, one of the older agents asked, "I understand that as of this time. You think that Charlie had taken one person and that she may be alive?"

Chance shook his head. "No. I believe he has taken two people, and I am not sure that any of them are…are alive. But we are hoping. He has given no indication that they have been killed, and he has always written to us to say when that's happened."

The man looked confused and reopened the case file. "I'm sorry. I'm only seeing two kidnappings listed in the report," the agent said.

"Yes, but as of last night, our officers who were watching Ms. Tina's house confirmed that she was not there and hadn't been in some time. All of Tina's family have said they have not heard from her. We are working under the opinion that Charlie witnessed her being questioned and has taken her in an attempt to keep her from being questioned further," Chance said, and seeing no other questions, he took his seat again.

"Thank you, Captain," said Turtle.

Tom spoke again. "All right, gentlemen, let's load up and meet at the tower this afternoon. We will wait until the lunch traffic has died down and moved in at that time. Monitor your phone for my directions." The men stood and started leaving in pairs again. When Chance had watched the last pair exit, he turned back to Tom and Turtle. "I'm going to have my detectives head over and make sure the top floor is cleared. Did you want me to have them sit on the door?"

Tom shook his head. "No, that's all right. I already have the building manager monitoring the security feed. But go ahead and have them clear the floor, just to make sure nobody is hiding anywhere."

Chance agreed and yelled out to Merrings, "Grab Truman and meet me in my office."

After a quick meeting with the Captain, Merrings and Truman left to grab their coats. The snow had not let up for the last few days, and it was going to be a slow drive over to the tower. True to their prediction, the streets were still being plowed free of snow, leaving a thick sheet of ice that the salt had not melted.

Merrings drove in silence, trying to concentrate on not sliding through intersections, while Truman looked through his phone. "You know, I have had no luck on this dating app," he said with disgust. "I don't think that girls even know what they want."

Merrings grinned. "No messages yet?" he asked.

"No! And I like messaging all of them. You know like throwing everything against a wall and seeing what I hit."

Merrings laughed out loud. "You are ridiculous, dude! Girls can smell how desperate you are through their phones!"

Truman turned off his phone. "I'm not desperate!" he grumped.

It took twice as long as they expected, but eventually, they pulled up safely in front of the tower. Making their way to the elevator, it was a surprisingly quick ride to the top floor. Drawing their weapons, they stepped carefully out of the doors. The floor was brightly lit from the windows that surrounded it on all sides. With a bar, two bathrooms, and two larger main rooms to clear, they signaled to each other as to who would be stepping through first in each room. Merrings took his turn first and carefully opened the men's bathroom before stepping in. Finding nothing, he signaled it as clear, and they moved on to the women's bathroom. Finding nothing again, they moved the opening of the largest of the two main rooms. Inside, they could see card tables had been set up for an upcoming party.

Stepping inside, they split apart and began clearing between each table. After ten minutes of searching the floor, it became apparent that no one was hiding anywhere. Merrings and Truman holstered their pistols and began looking for anything that looked out of place. Truman walked out of site, while Merrings took a look under the poker tables for anything. Nothing stood out to him as odd, so he walked out to search the bathrooms. Right before he was about to look in the women's, he heard Truman call out, "Hey! Come check this out!"

Merrings joined Truman behind the bar. There, on the floor mat behind the sink, were two wet footprints, but more importantly, clear as day was a set of very clear fingerprints on the stainless-steel faucet. Merrings smiled and made a call to the station. It wouldn't be too long before there was a team here to get the fingerprints. With any luck, they could compare them to the fingerprints they had gotten from Charlie's room. They waited until the team arrived and collected the foot and fingerprints. Then they followed the men out and headed back to the station to await the results.

At one-thirty the FBI arrived to set up their equipment. In all corners of the room, agents were hiding cameras in plants and under tables. Chance, who had decided to tag along, watched in amazement. He had never seen cameras so small, and the fact that they were wireless was shocking, but the technicians assured him the pictures would be very clear. Two men carried a drone to the roof in a very large plastic case; Chance followed. A few agents had already gone ahead and set up a small heater and placed it inside the elevator control room for the men who would be controlling the drones. The men opened the case and started removing foam inserts, revealing something out of a science fiction movie. Each of its four arms had a propeller attached, and an array of cameras were attached underneath its gray fiberglass body.

"Why is it gray? I would have figured it would be black," Chance asked.

One of the agents explained, "It's been painted gray so it won't stand out against the sky. If it was black, it would only blend at night." Chance felt stupid but then reasoned that it wasn't like he ever had the opportunity to use something like that. Seeing that everything was in hand, he made his way back down the stairs.

Chance's phone rang as he was watching the agents work. He listened intently and smiled. Hanging up, he signaled for Tom to join him. "Hey, that was the lab. The prints match the ones we got from Charlie's apartment. He has been here. And it had to be within the past day because the footprints were still wet," he relayed.

Tom nodded and said, "Good, then we know he has intentions of actually being here tomorrow. We are almost done here. From here on out, we just watch and wait for him to make his move."

Chance nodded and watched him let the other agents know. "It won't be long," he said to no one in particular.

Chapter 38

The Sicilian Defense

Gershing had managed to get some fitful sleep in between bursts of pain but was awoken to the muffled moaning of the woman behind him. He wanted to call out to her, but he knew he couldn't. He shook his body, hoping the sound of the chains hitting the ground would bring her attention to him. Her muffled voice called out to him. He stopped deliberately and then quickly shook the chains again, hoping this would convey some form of communication to her. She sobbed out a muffled plea for help, and Gershing shook his chain twice. She sniffled and pulled herself to her feet. She strained against her bindings again, but they still did not give. Gershing tried to get her talking again by shaking his chains, but the chains were violently snatched out of his hands! A foot caught him solidly against his head, and he fell to the floor.

Annoyed, their captor rolled a cart into the room and loaded Gershing onto it. The gagged woman listened as he was rolled out of the room, and tears fell from her eyes. But it wouldn't be long until she heard the cart roll back into the room. Through the bottom of her blindfold, she could see hands grabbing her roughly and untying her from her post. She was pushed heavily onto the cart and rolled toward the door. She tossed herself off the cart and kicked her feet when the hands tried to pick her back up. The last thing she saw was a heavy boot swing at her face and then nothing. She awoke later in horrifying pain and felt the sticky blood that had mostly dried from her nose. She could smell the body odor of the man that she lay beside in the trunk of a now moving car. He had clearly defecated on himself, and she could smell a strong scent of urine. Not that she was any better; it had been days since she was allowed to use the bathroom and had urinated on herself as well. She gagged on the smell and would have thrown up if she had eaten anything for the last few days. For now, it was just dry heaving.

She listened as the car pulled up to and away from different intersections as it drove. What seemed like an hour went by until they pulled to a final stop and the trunk lid was lifted, allowing a flood of fresh air in. Gratefully she sat up, but she was dragged unceremoniously from the trunk and dumped on the floor. Fearful of being kicked in the face again, she lay there obediently until she was loaded back onto the small cart and rolled away.

The cart rumbled down a warm hallway until a squeaky door was opened. A very pungent, acidic smell hung in the room's air. Hands pulled her onto her feet, and she was guided to a chair to sit down and was tied securely to it. The door closed, and the woman tried to make sense of where she was. It wasn't long before she was joined by the man and their captor. She pleaded for mercy and to be let go, but it fell on deaf ears. The door closed, leaving them in the dark room alone.

Outside, Charlie looked up at the looming tower in awe. He had walked past it a hundred times but never had he appreciated its design until that night. The snowfall framed the dark building in simplistic beauty, and Charlie suddenly was awash in renewed hope. He took in a deep breath and pulled on his gloves. He had work to do. The trunk wasn't going to empty itself. Whistling, he got back in his car and drove into the parking garage below the building.

Chapter 39

The End Is Nigh

The big night had finally come. Chance nervously rubbed his hands and watched the cameras from the surveillance van that was parked just up the street from the tower. As of yet, no one had come to the top floor, but Chance had a feeling that it was all about to come to an end. The entire day, he was consumed with his fear that Aryn was in Charlie's hands. He hoped she wasn't hurt, and he felt this was his last chance to get her back.

Tom and Turtle took turns watching the front of the building with binoculars. The last of the building's employees had left about an hour before, and no one had driven into the parking garage or tried to get into any of its several entrances. The radio hissed, and a voice confirmed that the drone was active and flying overhead.

Chance sighed and shuffled a bit in his seat. It could be a long night, and he didn't want to be stiff, in case he had to move quickly. He checked that his weapon had a round chambered and slid it back into his shoulder holster. Turtle watched him in silence but was secretly worried about him. He had watched the stress bear down on Chance for the past few weeks, and it had worn him down. It was clear that Chance had not slept for several nights, as his eyes were sunken in and bloodshot. He handed Chance a cup of coffee, which he accepted gratefully.

Hours passed, and Chance looked at his watch. He was starting to lose hope as he watched the seconds tick by. It was already a quarter till three, and they hadn't seen any change. He stepped out of the cab and leaned against the side of the van and lit a cigarette. As he took a long draw, he was joined by Tom, who leaned beside him but said nothing. Chance lit another cigarette and offered it to the man. Tom put the offered cigarette to his lips and nodded. Still nothing was said. Nothing had to be. Both men knew what was on the line, and talking about it wouldn't make it happen any faster. Just two, veteran law enforcement officers, understanding each other.

Finished, Chance flipped his cigarette butt into the street and was just about to step back into the van when a loud alarm sounded from the tower! Confused, he left the door open for Tom to climb in and asked what was happening. Turtle waved at him to be quiet and listened intently to the radio set on his head. Chance poked his head around Turtle and looked at the video monitors. There, in vivid color, was a fire raging in what looked like the sink of the bar. Sprinklers rained down onto the top floor. "What's going on?" he demanded again. Turtle took off his headset and handed it to Tom before explaining excitedly "We aren't sure yet, the sink just burst out on fire. According to the monitors no one went in."

Chance didn't wait for anything more and jumped out of the van. He drew his weapon as he ran toward the building. The elevators inside had been automatically shut down for safety, so he was forced to take the stairs. Thirty floors he ran, breathing heavily the entire way. Tom and Turtle were close behind. Finally, they came to the top floor, and he threw open the door, gun drawn.

Inside agents were struggling to put out the last of the sink fire with a fire extinguisher. The sprinkler system still rained down on them as they tried to make sense of what had happened. Chance cursed and slammed the palm of his fist against the wall. How did this happen? One of the agents kicked open the cabinet beneath the sink and let the smoke clear, before looking in with his flashlight. "It looks like some sort of incendiary device was attached to the garbage disposal," he informed everyone. Chance cursed again.

Charlie was one step ahead of them. But what was the point? Just to mess with them? He walked back to join Tom and whispered,

"Look, I didn't see a phone attached to the device, which means he's got to be with the area to have set it off, right?"

Tom considered this and then jogged over to the other agents and started barking orders then he jogged back to Chance to update him. "My guys are going to start on this floor and work their way down and clear the building. I thought you and Turtle would want to join me and we can start at the bottom. Work our way up, you know?" Eagerly Chance agreed and led the men down to the basement via the stairwell.

On the first floor, Charlie whistled and tossed a detonator back in his bag. It was astonishing what you could make with stuff from a hardware store and a RadioShack. He walked back down the stairs to the basement and flipped off the lights again. Bending down, he grabbed an extremely heavy bag and dragged it down the hall toward an empty room. But as he made his way toward the mechanical room, he could smell a very distinct acid smell. His curiosity piqued, and he dropped the bag and started smelling different doors until he found the one that the smell was clearly coming from. He went back and dragged the bag back with him. Carefully, he opened the door and stepped inside. Before he realized it, the back of a shovel slammed into his face. He fell to the floor with a *thunk*. Blood seeping into a pool beneath his head and leached into his hair.

Behind him, his attacker struggled with the bag, pulling it into the room, and closed the door.

Chapter 40

The Coda

Chance took the lead when they entered the basement and began by checking the first door to see if it was locked. Jiggling it he indicated that it was, and Turtle reached into his pocket to get the keys that the building manager had given them. After unlocking the door, he returned to the rear of their three-man line and waited for the signal to enter. Careful not to throw his silhouette into the frame of the door, he opened it and stepped in carefully. The two men quickly entered behind him and scanned their weapons across the darkened room. Tom felt the wall until he felt the light switch. Flicking the lights on, they moved through the boiler room cautiously. Each shadow made their heart race. But meeting at the rear of the room it was apparent that no one was hiding. "Let's move on to the next room," Chance said.

Tom nodded and then stopped and listened to his earpiece. He acknowledged the silent voice in his ear and said, "They have the exits secure on the building and no one has left the building." Chance nodded and returned to the hall to search the next room. Even though he was with two men he trusted, he was nervous. More nervous than any other time in his life. The hallway light flickered, and the men silently approached the next room. Outside, they could smell a very strong odor. Chance checked the door; it was unlocked. He signaled to the two men and opened the door. He stepped through into the darkroom. Suddenly, the door slammed shut behind him, and he could hear something heavy falling against the metal door.

Outside, Tom threw his weight against the door, to no avail. "Something's against it!" he said angrily. Turtle pounded on the door and demanded that it was opened. No answer came, but two gunshots rang out, one of which hit the door with a loud clang. The men ducked to the side of the door and radioed for the agents upstairs to join them.

Inside, Chance fired back at the door. The muzzle flash blinded him momentarily, and he walked slowly back toward the door, feeling for the light switch on the wall. Something slammed into his wrist, knocking the pistol from his grip, and he fell to the floor and screamed in pain! The lights flickered on, and Chance struggled to his knees as eyes adjusted. A blurry figure stood, just out of reach, in front of him. He backed away and blinked his eyes. When he opened them, he was shocked to see the face of Aryn!

Chance knelt there in shock, unable to form words. She smiled and walked back to the center of the room. Against the wall was a man tied and bound, his face and hair stained red. Beside him was a man missing an arm. Chance crawled over to him and checked for life, the faint sign of a pulse, and shallow breathing came from his unconscious body. He turned the man's face toward him. There in the crumpled pile before him lay Charlie.

The man who was tied up on the wall gasped for air loudly, sending waves of fear through Chance's body. He turned quickly and leaned in to check and see if he was okay. The man nodded and then pointed his head toward the opposite wall; Gershing lay in front of a barrel of some sort. He wasn't moving; his now unbandaged sockets made him look like some sort of flesh-colored skull.

"Aryn? I don't understand?" he asked, bewildered. She smiled and slowly walked toward him. In her hand, she held his own service pistol that she had recovered from the floor.

"I'm not surprised, lover," she said sarcastically. "You haven't understood anything that Charlie or I have done. He even told you that he didn't kill the whores, and you didn't even entertain the idea that there was a second killer!" Chance stood slowly to his feet, but

Aryn pointed the pistol at him and then back down on the floor. Obediently, he knelt back down.

"But I've known you since high school," he mumbled.

"Did you, though? Did you, really? How much time did you spend with poor, geeky Aryn? The school paper editor, the girl who didn't develop until after she graduated? No! You didn't know me! You were the popular one, the varsity wrestler, the football star! I know you, though!" she snarled. The metal door thumped because of the agents outside kicking it, but it held firm.

"But why kill those girls?" he asked.

"Um, well, and I don't remember inviting you to interrupt me, but if you really want to know…that was for Charlie." And she pointed in the direction of the men that Chance had checked. "I have read about murders happening in this city for years, and you all never saw the connection! But I did. I don't even know how you missed it? It was *so* obvious! Every one of them were rapists, child molesters, or murderers. It read like you had your own personal superhero here in Dayton. The more I read, the more I liked him. Finally, a man who only wanted to do good! Who didn't care about his popularity or what people thought about him. He only saw right and wrong." She swooned.

Chance lowered himself into a sitting position and rubbed his wrist, trying to think of a way out of this. "But I loved you," he said.

She openly laughed. "Well, that's really nice of you! In a lot of ways, I cared about you too, but I only can love one man." She walked over to the barrel and put her hand on the top. "And now we can. I got rid of the last thing that kept us apart." She grabbed a gold watch off of the top of the barrel and tossed to Chance's feet. He picked it up and turned it over. On the back were inscribed the words "I love you, Tammy."

He put it back on the ground and asked, "Who's Tammy?"

Behind him, the man on the wall moaned, clearly in pain. She rolled her eyes but explained, "Oh, she was the love of his life until I caught her cheating. Now she's just another thing out of the way so we can be together."

Chance tried standing again. This time, she allowed it. "Where is Tammy now?" he asked.

She thumped the top of the barrel. "What a great question! She is right here," she said with an evil smile.

"Is she dead?" he asked.

"Not when I put her in, but yeah, I am pretty sure she is dead now." She laughed maniacally then continued, "She screamed when I dropped her into the Fluoroantimonic acid. They say it can strip the DNA out of a body in just hours. Shall we find out?" she asked and then pushed the barrel onto its side, letting its contents splash across the floor in a pool of red pulp. Half of what Chance could only assume was a skull rolled toward him. He grimaced and swallowed the bile that rushed up into his mouth.

Aryn, careful to avoid the pool of acid, stepped around to another barrel and leaned against it. "Don't worry, I saved one more barrel for you, lover."

He backed away slowly until his back was against the wall. Looking around him, he searched frantically for a weapon; finally, his eyes fell on a can of kerosene that had been placed behind one of the workbenches.

"But why kill the prostitutes?" he asked, hoping to distract her from her task.

She frowned. "Really? I would have thought that was obvious. The girls were just a way to draw out Charlie. If he knew someone was blaming him for the killings, he would try to find me. But your cops kept getting in the way, which is where Rashan came in."

Chance raised his head in disbelief. "You killed him?"

She kicked Gershing as she passed him. He cried out in pain. "Yeah, I did. I did that just for you. Well, kind of for you. Charlie seemed to like you, so in a way, I did it for him. Charlie doesn't deserve to be chased by just a detective, he's worth more than that! It was only fitting that he be chased by the head of the police department. Maybe it's the writer in me, but I made sure that he recognized me before he died," she said with a smile. "Oh, and his wife—well, you should know I made it quick for her."

Chance had never felt such rage! He had been betrayed by the woman he loved, and she stood before him telling him that she had killed a person he admired so casually.

He sidestepped slowly toward the table as she aimed the gun at his head. His leg hit the side and he feigned like he was cowering away from her and crouched down. "Any last words, honey?" she asked sweetly.

He turned himself so that his side was to her and said, "Yeah, go to hell!" and he threw the can at her head. A shot rang out, and a bullet struck the cinderblock by his head. He ducked and charged at her. In his haste, he spilled the kerosene all over the two of them in their struggle. She kicked at his face until she had successfully freed herself and recovered the gun. Pulling herself to her knees, she aimed the gun at Chance again and pulled the trigger, shooting him in the shoulder. Hot scorching pain tore through him. He fell to the ground. She took aim again and tightened her finger on the trigger. But before she could shoot, she heard the sound of Zippo being lit. There standing behind her was the man that was previously tied against the wall, holding the Zippo that had fallen from Chance's pocket during their struggle. He wiped the blood from his eyes and with one angry movement threw the lighter onto her gas-soaked jacket. With a scream, she frantically clawed at her burning flesh.

Chance watched her roll across the floor in agony. He picked up the gun and in an act of mercy pulled the trigger. His eyes filled with tears as he walked to the door to let the agents in.

Men flooded in. But all they found was three wounded men and the burnt corpse of Aryn lying in the center of the room. Tom took Chance to a corner and took a look at his shoulder. "Looks like a flesh wound, nothing too bad. Here hold this against it while we get an ambulance over here." He said and pressed a handkerchief into the wound. Chance winced in pain but nodded. He watched as agents checked the other men and started to apply first aid.

Turtle walked over. "It looks like everyone is going to make it except for the guy with no arm." He informed Chance. "That's Charlie," Chance said and then blacked out.

Chapter 41

The Aftermath

Chance opened his eyes and stared at the hospital ceiling from his bed. It had been twelve hours since Aryn had died, and the wounds she left in her wake were being taken care of by medical staff. Gershing had been returned to the ICU, and the man that had helped him with Aryn was sharing a room with Chance, only separated by a curtain.

"Hey, how are you doing, Captain?" a voice asked through his drug-induced stupor. He turned his head lazily to the side to see Pullman, Merrings, and Truman standing beside his bed. He nodded indicating he was all right.

"Good, boss. Just wanted to let you know, we confirmed that the body with no arm was Charlie. The coroner sent back the fingerprint match an hour ago. It's over, we got him."

Merrings said and laid his hand on Chance's arm. It was over. Chance closed his eyes, and a tear fell from it. It wasn't over for him. He would always see Aryn's face when he closed his eyes. The detectives felt awkward seeing their friend crying and said their goodbyes. After they left, he sobbed quietly to himself until a voice came from the other side of the curtain "I'm sorry. She must have meant a lot to you."

Chance wiped his eyes and took a labored breath. "Yeah, thanks."

The man continued, "I recently lost someone I loved too. I imagine it will stay with us for a while."

Chance said nothing, and the man's voice fell silent. Eventually, the medication took complete hold of him and he faded off to sleep.

When he awoke, he could hear his monitor beeping in rhythm with his heartbeat. Looking down at his shoulder, he could see that the dressing had been changed again. He tried to force himself into a sitting position, but a nurse rushed over and pushed him back down gently. "Please lay back down, sir," she said and then checked his vitals on the monitor.

An hour passed, and Tom walked in to see how he was doing. Chance chatted with him a bit and then pushed the call button on the bed. "Look before I head back to Washington. I wanted to thank you for being so accommodating. You didn't have to be, and we appreciate it. I understand you got some convalescent leave coming up. You ought to take some of it and come see us if you get the chance," Tom said.

"No way. If I'm going anywhere it's to the Bahamas!" Chance said with a chuckle.

Tom smiled and shook Chance's good hand. "See you around."

The tired captain closed his eyes again and faded off to sleep once again. He slept the kind of sleep one can only get from medication. Dreamless, deep, restful. It was so deep that he was only slightly awakened two hours later by doctors barking orders and rushing down the hall. Something had driven them to a frenzy. Outside, police sirens approached and footsteps ran past his curtain. He was aware of all of this but only partially registered it, as he was still half asleep. Try as he might to fight it, he fell back into his deep sleep.

A hand reached out and roughly shook him awake. "What. What's going on?" he asked, still half-asleep.

Truman squeezed his arm. "Captain, it's Gershing. He's dead! Captain, can you hear me?" he asked loudly.

Chance shook his head to clear it of the cobwebs. "What's going on?" he asked again.

"Somebody smothered Gershing with a pillow. Gershing's dead!" Truman said again with more urgency.

"We have to get you and your roommate over there to safety!" Chance nodded and swung his legs to the ground. His legs gave out a bit, and Truman swung his arm around Chance's waist to stabilize him. Once he regained his balance, he reached out and pulled the white curtain back that separated the two men from each other. The bed was empty. The only thing that remained was a medical bracelet. Chance picked up and looked at it. There on the name line in block print was "Charlie."

Chapter 42

And the Curtains Close

Charlie leaned over and kissed Tina on the cheek as she drove. She smiled and squeezed his hand. "I'm so glad you're okay." Charlie nodded and squeezed her hand back reassuringly. "I will always come back to you, princess." They rode for several blocks in silence while Charlie reflected on everything. The police had everything they needed to close the case on him. A body they believed to be his and Aryn's confession. And with Gershing now dead, Charlie felt like he had completed his work. It was true that he would miss Tammy, but having Tina beside him eased the pain he felt in his heart.

"I think we should take a vacation while the heat dies down," Charlie said to Tina.

"Where to?" she asked with a smile. He looked out the window and grinned. "The Bahamas."

About the Author

Joshua Burkheiser, born on a border town in Arizona, attended Wright State University, where he majored in psychology. Currently, he calls Dayton, Ohio, home. A father of two, he retired from the US Army in 2013 and continues to work in the Federal Service. While researching the city he lives in he was inspired by a series of murders that plagued Ohio in the late '80s and '90s. This inspiration led him to develop the character Charlie.

CPSIA information can be obtained
at www.ICGtesting.com
Printed in the USA
BVHW030127300921
617837BV00006B/82

9 781638 601500